AMERICAN ADVENTURES

Luke
on the High Seas

---•---

MORE AMERICAN ADVENTURES

Luke
1849—On the Golden Trail

Joseph
1861—A Rumble of War

Thomas

Thomas in Danger

AMERICAN ADVENTURES

Luke
on the High Seas

BONNIE PRYOR

ILLUSTRATED BY
BERT DODSON

HarperCollins*Publishers*

Library of Congress Cataloging-in-Publication Data

Pryor, Bonnie.
Luke on the High Seas / Bonnie Pryor; illustrated by Bert Dodson.
p. cm.—(American adventures)
Sequel to: Luke, 1849—on the golden trail.
Summary: In 1850, Luke and Toby set sail from Boston to California on a voyage featuring shady characters, a story of a lost gold mine, and a cabin boy with a secret.
ISBN 0-688-17134-6
[1. Sea stories.   2. Mystery and detective stories.]   I. Dodson, Bert, ill.
II. Title.   PZ7.P94965 Lw 2000   [Fic]—dc21   99-46226

10   9   8   7   6   5   4   3   2

❖

First Edition

Contents

ONE Preparing for Adventure. 1

TWO The *Eagle* 9

THREE Saying Good-bye. 17

FOUR The Journey Begins 24

FIVE Practical Jokes 34

SIX Jim's Story 47

SEVEN Becalmed 56

EIGHT Neptune's Visit. 63

NINE Secrets 73

TEN Land Ho! 81

ELEVEN Rio 90

TWELVE Pirates. 100

THIRTEEN Shipwreck 108

FOURTEEN Rounding the Cape 119

FIFTEEN Attack! 129

SIXTEEN Shark 137

SEVENTEEN Taking Back the *Eagle* 151

More about *Luke on the High Seas*. 161

ONE

—◆—

Preparing for Adventure

Mr. Appleby rapped sharply on the desk with his ruler. "Luke Reed," he said, "are you daydreaming again?"

From the second-floor windows of his uncle's large brick house, Luke had a perfect view of Boston Harbor. But gazing out, he'd been remembering the view from the tiny window of his own family's sod house in Iowa. There all he could see was endless, flat miles of tall prairie grass.

Luke focused on the large map spread out before him, and he sighed. "Sorry, Mr. Appleby. Geography gives me a headache."

Toby gave him a sympathetic glance, but Mr. Appleby only frowned. "You are far behind other boys your age. I promised your uncle that I would help you catch up."

Luke flushed as he picked up his pen and went back to work. Uncle Eli had given him his first chance at schooling. At home the nearest school had been miles away, and his father had needed his help on the farm. It was only because a hailstorm and a fire had ruined this year's crops that his father had finally allowed him to travel with his uncle to Boston.

Mr. Appleby tapped his ruler on the desk a second time. In return for tutoring Luke and Toby, he was to receive free passage to California when Uncle Eli's ship, the *Eagle*, set sail in a week.

The pale, bespectacled tutor didn't seem the sort to go prospecting for gold in California. But this was 1850, and the entire country was struck with gold fever. More than a hundred men had already paid for their passage on the *Eagle*, hoping to find gold at the end of the journey. Uncle Eli wasn't going to look for gold, though. He hoped to make his fortune by selling the goods packed into the cargo hold of his ship.

Everything was right on schedule except for

signing up a crew. So many men had already left Boston that Captain Andrews had to comb the streets, looking for experienced sailors.

Luke bent over his map, tracing the journey he would soon make. From Boston they would sail south, past the eastern coast of the United States and continuing across the equator. Except for a few islands, they would not see land again until they reached Rio de Janeiro, a city on the coast of Brazil. They would rest there for about a week, his uncle promised, because the next leg of the journey would be the worst. From Rio they would sail around the tip of South America, known for wild storms and rough water, before they headed north to California.

Luke filled in the names of all the countries he could remember. At last he finished the assignment and waited while Mr. Appleby checked his answers.

"Much better," the tutor said at last. "Only one mistake today." He pointed to a large island near the tip of Florida. "This island is called Cuba."

Mr. Appleby checked Toby's history assignment. "Excellent as usual," he said with a pleased nod.

Toby's mother was Uncle Eli's housekeeper.

Although many people had slaves, Uncle Eli had given Toby and his mother their freedom. They lived in a small house at the back of Uncle Eli's estate. Since the day the boys had met three months ago, they had been fast friends.

"You are free for the day," Mr. Appleby announced. Luke and Toby jumped up so quickly they nearly knocked over their chairs and thundered down the stairs to the kitchen.

Colleen met them at the kitchen door. Her hands were at her waist, and a stern look crossed the cook's usually smiling face. "And don't you two sound like a herd of cattle coming down those stairs. Lucky for you Miss Maisie has gone to do a bit of shopping. She'd not tolerate such ungentlemanly behavior."

Miss Maisie was Toby's mother.

The boys hung their heads, but Luke peeked up enough to notice the twinkle in Colleen's eyes and to see her assistant, Lettie, giggling silently in the corner by the bake ovens.

"Saints preserve us, we ought to be horsewhipped," Toby said in an easy imitation of Colleen's Irish brogue.

She laughed and snapped her towel at him. "None of your sass, young man, or you'll not be getting any of the cherry pie I made this morning. Now you two sit there at the table."

Luke sat meekly as he was ordered. Colleen served them a big plate of boiled beef cooked with cabbage and potatoes. Dessert was, as she had promised, a huge piece of cherry pie.

"That was wonderful," Luke said, finally pushing himself away from the table.

"Has word come from your parents?" Colleen asked as she started washing the dishes.

Luke nodded. His face clouded with homesickness for a moment as he thought of his parents and brothers and sisters back home. None of them could read or write, but Mr. Kline at the general store had written down the letter. "Father isn't too pleased at my wanting to go to California, but he hopes I'll get tired of traveling and want to come home."

"You've already done more traveling than most folks ever do." Toby counted on his fingers. "Let's see. Just to come to Boston, you traveled by horseback, barge, stagecoach, and train."

"Do you think your father is right?" Colleen dried her hands on her apron and waited for Luke's answer.

"I do miss my family," Luke said honestly, "but there are so many things to see."

"And draw," Toby added. "I never saw a fellow so determined to draw everything he sees."

Colleen put her arm around Luke's shoulders. "Luke here is going to be a famous painter someday."

Luke blushed, but Toby nodded. "I think so, too. Did your father like the picture you painted of your uncle's ship?" he asked.

"Pa said he was going to pin it to the wall in the new house they're building," Luke answered. "Since he doesn't much approve of a fellow wanting to be an artist, those are pretty strong words."

Not bothering with their coats, the boys raced out the door and down the cobblestone streets to the harbor. The October sky was gray, and the wind was brisk and cold. Luke hunched against the wind, which was sharp enough to take his breath away. "Seems like a dangerous time to set sail," Toby remarked. "We're bound to run into some storms this time of year."

"Uncle Eli says the seasons are reversed below the equator. If we leave now, we'll be at Cape Horn in December. That's summer there, but even then the weather is rough."

Luke thought about the *Eagle*. Uncle Eli had bought the ship after she'd been damaged from running aground. For the last two months scores of workmen had scurried over her, repairing the hole in her side and overlapping new thin sheets of copper under the waterline. Uncle Eli had explained that this would keep borers and barnacles from attaching themselves and damaging the hull.

The ship was nearly restored to her former glory. No, even better, Luke thought. The inside had been completely refurbished. The stateroom walls were paneled in mahogany and oak. The floors were covered with new carpets from India, and on the walls hung beautiful tapestries from China. Even the lowliest seaman would find his berth spread with a new mattress, and the galley boasted brand-new pots and pans.

"Has your mother decided if she'll sail with us to California?" Luke asked Toby.

"One day she says yes, the next no," Toby

answered. "I just hope she doesn't change her mind about letting me go."

"Do you think she might?" Luke asked. The trip would not be nearly as much fun without his friend.

"She is awfully worried," Toby admitted. "Your uncle keeps telling her that it's a wonderful opportunity to see some of the world, and that Captain Andrews will allow no harm to come to us. But we'll be gone a long time, and to tell you the truth, I think she is afraid of the ocean."

"I didn't think Miss Maisie was afraid of anything." Luke chuckled. "The other day I heard her tell Uncle Eli he couldn't come into the house until he'd wiped his feet."

"What did he say?" Toby asked.

"He said, 'Madam, this is my house,' but your mama just looked him in the eye and said, 'I know whose house this is. And I know who keeps it clean. Now wipe those feet.'" Luke grinned, remembering. "Uncle Eli wiped his feet."

TWO

———◆———

The *Eagle*

The wind whipped the gray ocean, capping the waves with froth. In spite of this, the *Eagle* was a beehive of activity. Workmen scurried about with paintbrushes and tools while stevedores with bulging muscles carried crates and barrels of sugar, flour, boots, tools, shirts, underwear, and even furniture into the hold. Luke inhaled deeply. The sharp odors of tar, varnish, and paint nearly covered the fishy, salt scent of the sea.

"It even *smells* interesting," he remarked.

The *Eagle*, like all clipper ships, had a narrow hull. Uncle Eli had explained that the ship's design allowed her to move faster through the water. A huge carved eagle was fastened to the bow. With

its fierce eyes, hooked beak, and backswept wings, the eagle seemed poised to soar through the air, pulling the ship with it. A painter, suspended with a scaffolding, was applying a fresh coat of golden color to the wings. The ship bucked and rolled in the choppy waves. So much paint had splashed on the painter that he looked like a golden statue come to life.

Uncle Eli, looking every inch the prosperous Boston businessman, was admiring the effect. He gave the boys a cheery wave, and they boarded the ship together. Immediately Eli rolled up his shirtsleeves and was helping load a stack of barrels into the hold. While he worked, he sang in a loud, deep voice.

"That man sure likes to sing," Toby said, shaking his head.

Luke smiled. Uncle Eli's voice was loud but not always on key.

"You boys sand the rails on the poop deck," Uncle Eli called.

The boys groaned but went obediently to the stern, or rear of the ship where the poop deck rose high above the main deck. The ship rolled and heaved against the dock as they sanded the railing.

It was hard work made even worse by the numbing cold. "I think we've done enough," said Toby at last. He stood for a moment holding the wheel, pretending to be the helmsman.

"What's in that wooden box in front of you?" asked Luke.

"That's the binnacle box," Toby explained. "There's a compass in there and a lantern so the helmsman can see it at night." He rang the small bell fastened to the top of the box. "This is the ship's bell. That's how the sailors know when it's time for their watch."

"Uncle Eli says the captain will spend most of his time up here. From here he can see almost everything on the ship," Luke said. He stood on the edge of the deck facing forward, pretending he was the captain looking down on the main deck. Beyond that were the forecastle deck and the deckhouse with the crew's quarters.

Luke peeked through the saloon skylight jutting up from the deck. "Let's go inside. At least we'll be out of the cold."

They ducked inside the passageway to the first-class cabins. Toby looked a little pasty. The ship's movement was making his stomach churn. Somewhat reluctantly he followed Luke as they inspected the small but pleasant first-class passenger cabins. Each had two bunks, a chest of drawers, a small writing desk, and a chair. "I heard Uncle Eli say the first-class passengers paid five hundred and fifty dollars for their passage," Luke said.

Uncle Eli's stateroom was large and comfortably furnished. It opened into the large saloon filled with soft couches, chairs, and a desk. The skylight made the room airy and bright. The boys were to share a small room next door. Beyond that was a pantry. At one end was a small room not much bigger than a closet for the cabin boy. Beyond the pantry was a bathroom for the first-class passengers with a wooden tub for bathing.

The boys went down the stairs that led to the tween decks area where most of the passengers would stay. Rows of bunks were fitted along the walls, and there was a small dining area. Next came the galley with its huge stove and lockers for storing supplies. The sailors' quarters were even more crowded. The only light came from a whale oil lamp hung from the ceiling.

Suddenly something large and furry ran between Luke's legs. With a shriek he jumped back.

"W-what was that?" Toby stammered.

Two sailors were coming down the stairs with a large crate. They were wild, rough-looking men, and Luke backed away nervously. Then one of them smiled, showing a mouth of black and broken teeth. "I'll bet you just met George," he said. "He belongs to the captain."

"George?" Luke asked fearfully.

The sailor nodded his head toward a large water keg. A fine orange cat sat calmly watching them as he licked his paws.

Luke reached out and patted the cat's head, hoping the sailors couldn't see his still-shaking knees. George rubbed himself on Luke's hand, and a rumbling purr sounded in his throat.

"Have you made a decision about the voyage?" Uncle Eli asked Miss Maisie that evening.

Toby and Luke held their breaths waiting for her answer. "I'm nearly grown," Toby pleaded. "Lots of boys my age are already apprenticed to learn a trade."

"Twelve years old is hardly grown," Miss Maisie

said dryly. "Still, I don't want to deny you such a grand adventure. Mr. Reed has assured me that it will be a pleasant trip and that you will be safe on the *Eagle*. So I have decided to let you go."

Toby threw his arms around his mother, and she held him tight. "But I won't be going myself," she said finally. "I prefer to keep my feet on solid ground."

"Mama, are you sure?" Toby asked.

"Yes, I am," his mother answered.

"I will, of course, take good care of Toby," Uncle Eli promised. "But I wish you would change your mind and come with us."

Miss Maisie shook her head. "I've given it much thought. I know I would be miserable on board a ship. I get seasick in a rowboat! But I do have a suggestion. Perhaps Colleen should go. She is much more adventurous than I am."

"California! Me?" Colleen stared at them.

"That's a wonderful idea," Uncle Eli said. "The boys need a female hand to keep them in line, and we're still in need of a cook for the first-class passengers," he added. "It should be a pleasant voyage."

Both boys were fond of the petite Irishwoman with her sweet face and unfailingly cheerful disposition. The fact that she was a wonderful cook didn't make her less popular. Toby and Luke grabbed her hands and whirled her around. "Come with us, come with us," they sang.

Colleen laughed. "I'll do it," she said.

Uncle Eli smiled as she swirled past. "Make a list of what you need," he said.

"Chickens," she said immediately. "And goats. You'll be glad enough when you have a fresh egg and a glass of milk for breakfast."

Suddenly Uncle Eli began to sing. "Oh, we're bound for California, the chickens, goats, and me." Laughing, the others joined in his song. "And I hope by the time we get there, I will learn to sing on key."

THREE

Saying Good-bye

Six days later a large crowd gathered on the waterfront to bid farewell to their loved ones sailing on the *Eagle*. Even the cold wind and wild gray skies did little to dampen the crowd's spirits. Most seemed determined to present a cheerful front to the voyagers, although as the time for departure grew near, more and more tearful faces could be seen. Family members offered last-minute advice and good-bye hugs, and the passengers carried boxes and bags onto the ship and settled into their assigned spaces.

Most of the passengers had formed the Boston Mining Company, agreeing to share equipment and expenses and to band together once they had reached California. Uncle Eli was pleased that there were two doctors in the company. There were also shop owners, college professors, farmers, carpenters, even a judge.

Since all the berths had been sold, it had been necessary to partition off a section of Uncle Eli's sitting room to make a space for Colleen. Luke and Toby had helped, and now they proudly showed off their labors.

"Isn't this grand!" she had said, putting down her luggage. "It is certainly nothing like when I crossed the Atlantic from Ireland. Steerage was damp and smelly, everyone crowded together so you could hardly breathe."

Colleen shook her head as if to clear the terrible journey from her head. "You two better go on deck and watch all the excitement. I want to make a last-minute check of the pantry."

"All the chickens and goats are on board," Luke told her. "Uncle Eli built some cages and pens right on the deck."

Toby laughed. "I don't think they're happy about an ocean voyage. You should hear the commotion."

The boys went back into the passageway to head

for the upper decks. Suddenly the door to Uncle Eli's cabin opened, and a tall, thin, well-dressed man stepped out. "I was looking for the owner of this vessel," he said.

"Uncle Eli is on deck helping everyone get organized," Luke said. "Those are his private rooms."

"A gentleman on deck directed me here," explained the man. He paused at the sound of humming coming from the pantry. "Did I just hear a woman's voice?"

"Oh, that was Colleen," Toby answered. "She's going to cook for the first-class passengers."

The man squeezed by and opened the door to the pantry. Colleen turned from the well-packed cupboards. "Can I help you?" she asked.

"Sorry to bother you," the man said as he backed out of the door. "I thought you might be someone I knew."

"You say the owner is on deck?" the man asked. When Luke nodded, he brushed past them and climbed the stairs.

The boys followed and saw him talking urgently to Uncle Eli on deck. The man took a large white handkerchief from his pocket and dabbed at his eyes. Then the boys lost sight of him in the rush of passengers hurrying on and off the ship, purchasing last-minute supplies at the many shops along the waterfront. The first mate checked their names off as they finally settled in. Then Captain Andrews took a roll call of the crew and discovered that two were missing. His face turned beet red under his woolly beard. "Where's that cabin boy?" he shouted.

A slight figure with a dirty face and ragged pants ran to the captain.

"Look in every grogshop on the street," the captain roared. "Find those two men. They'd better be here before sailing if they know what's good for them."

The boy darted off. Luke watched until he was lost in the crowd. "That cabin boy doesn't look much older than we are," he remarked.

Toby shivered, remembering that only a few months before a sailor had tried to kidnap him and force him to be a cabin boy.

It took the boys some time to find Miss Maisie in the crowd. She gave Toby a kiss. "Keep up with your studies," she told him. She wiped her eyes with a handkerchief. Then she hugged Luke. "Watch out for each other."

Colleen had come on deck to watch the festivities. She wrapped her cloak tightly around her against the wind and blowing rain. "Don't you worry," she said. "I'll keep a good eye on them."

The boys waved as Miss Maisie returned to the dock.

"What an exciting day!" said a pleasant voice beside them. Luke saw a pudgy, balding man with a short beard and friendly gray eyes. "I'm Judge Jonas Myer," he said with a sweeping bow to Colleen. "Most people just call me Judge. I didn't know there was going to be a lady on board. And such a lovely one at that."

Colleen giggled a little at the judge's flattery. Toby rolled his eyes at Luke, and the two boys wandered off. They found Uncle Eli watching Captain Andrews as he assigned duties to the crew. Just then the two missing sailors scrambled aboard, looking a bit worse for wear from their night on the town. Captain Andrews scowled fiercely at them as they took their places in line.

"I'm glad I'm not one of those sailors," Toby said. "Captain Andrews looks mean."

"He has to be tough to handle the crew," Uncle Eli answered. "They are a pretty rough bunch."

"Who was that man you were talking to on the deck?" Luke asked.

"His name is Mr. Browning. He was trying to book a last-minute passage. Said his brother was sick and he wanted to get to California to care for him. I told him there was no room, but Mr. Appleby offered to share his cabin."

"We could use a few extra hands to search for stowaways," Captain Andrews announced loudly. Some of the men had already gone below, but Mr. Browning, the judge, and several others stepped forward. Captain Andrews divided the men. He sent the largest group to the hold.

"Look for anything unusual," Captain Andrews told them, "a box out of place or a barrel not properly sealed."

"What'll we do if we find someone?" asked one of the men.

"Just bring him to me," the captain said grimly.

Luke was sure Captain Andrews would not be

easy on anyone trying to get a free passage to California. He was relieved when the men found nothing suspicious.

At last, late in the afternoon, a tiny paddle-wheeled tug pulled them out into the harbor. The boys leaned over the rail and waved at Miss Maisie until she was a dot on the shoreline.

Toby's eyes were filled with tears. Luke understood how he felt. Even with the excitement of the journey it was hard to leave your family.

FOUR

The Journey Begins

A brisk wind was blowing. Even though there was a threat of a storm, the sails were unfurled, and the journey began. The boys tried to keep out of the way as the crew set the sails. The first mate, Mr. Levering, called out the orders. He was a handsome man, but his eyes were small and hard. Captain Andrews seemed to be everywhere, shouting orders sometimes, watching silently at other times. The ordinary sailors were a scruffy, dirty bunch, but they seemed to know just what to do. They scrambled over the rigging, singing as they worked, and the ship came to life with creaks and groans. Over all the other noises were the hum of wind in the rigging and the flapping of sails.

Even the smells were exciting, Luke thought. Closing his eyes, he identified the salty, fish smell of the ocean; the tar coming from the rigging; and the sharp, smoky scent of the stove in the galley burning off its new coat of paint.

A few of the passengers had remained on deck, but the cold soon drove most of them below.

"I hope we can stay ahead of this storm," Uncle Eli said. With a worried look he glanced up at the black clouds thickening in the sky.

Luke was shivering. "I think you boys'd better go to your cabin before you take a chill," Uncle Eli said. "At any rate I think Mr. Appleby is looking for you."

"Already?" Luke groaned. "I thought we would have one day without lessons."

Uncle Eli laughed. "You may be glad to have lessons to break the boredom before the voyage is over."

Luke could not imagine ever feeling bored. With the choppy sea and the rocking motion of the ship, just trying to walk was a challenge.

"It will take a few days to get your sea legs." Uncle Eli smiled as he watched Luke grab a rail to steady himself.

The boys went below and spent some time putting their clothes away in a small chest. Mr. Appleby had already left several lessons stacked neatly on the desk. Ignoring the lessons for now, they tossed a coin to see who would get the bottom bunk. Luke ended up on the top, which suited him fine. Toby sat down on his bunk. "I don't feel so good," he said.

Luke had been trying to convince himself that he was not getting seasick, but his stomach was churning with every roll of the ship.

There was a soft knock at the door. "It's Jim, the cabin boy. Miss Colleen says to come to the saloon for tea," said a muffled voice.

Luke opened the door. The cabin boy was dressed in rough clothing two or three sizes too big, and his hair was crudely cut. He ducked his head as he repeated his message so Luke couldn't quite make out his face in the dark passageway. Luke supposed the boy was shy. He thought of saying something friendly, but before he could speak the boy turned and walked back to Captain Andrews's room.

"I was going to ask him if he wanted to play

checkers or something when he wasn't working," Luke said.

"Good idea," Toby said. "It's nice that there's someone else our age on board."

Luke opened the door to the saloon. He was surprised to see it crowded with passengers. Uncle Eli had called a meeting to get things organized. The two doctors agreed to treat sick passengers, and a small area was assigned to be the hospital. Books were pooled together to make a lending library, and Mr. Appleby promised to keep track and make sure books were returned. Several volunteers with musical ability agreed to practice together with the idea of presenting some entertainment on Saturday nights, and Mr. Lane, who had been a divinity student, agreed to conduct church services on Sunday morning.

Colleen appeared from the pantry with a heavy tray piled with cups of tea and cakes. The teacups rattled as she tried to balance herself with the rolling of the ship.

Luke and the judge started toward her to help, but their way was blocked by the biggest man Luke had ever seen. "That's much too heavy for a little thing like you," he said in a soft voice. The giant grabbed the tray and held it while Colleen passed out the cups. Luke heard him tell Colleen that he was a carpenter and his name was Beardsly.

By the time the meeting ended, the sea was so rough that it was nearly impossible to balance a cup of tea without spilling the contents. Many of the passengers had already excused themselves and, looking miserable, returned to their berths.

"Captain Andrews says we are heading into a pretty bad storm," Uncle Eli said. "I want you boys to stay off the decks until it calms down. The sailors will be busy, and there is the danger of being washed overboard."

"What about the goats and the chickens?" Toby asked. Uncle Eli had given the job of caring for the animals to Luke and Toby.

"Give them some feed, and make sure the doors to their pens are tightly closed," Uncle Eli said. "Be quick, before the storm gets any worse."

The boys climbed down through the between decks quarters and into the hold, where several sacks of corn were stored.

George rubbed against Luke's leg. "That cat sure has taken a liking to you," Toby said.

"My father says I have a way with animals," Luke said, pausing to pat George's head.

Luke and Toby filled several containers and made their way upstairs. George followed until they opened the hatch door to the main deck, and seawater from the high waves sprayed in. With an unhappy meow George disappeared below.

"George has the right idea," Toby said. "Let's hurry."

Nodding, Luke led the way to the two large pens built in a sheltered corner. By the time they finished feeding the nervous animals, the storm was sending wave after wave splashing over the forecastle deck.

"I see why the captain stands on the poop deck," Luke said. "The stern stays a lot drier."

"I heard your uncle say that the waves coming over the deck make the sailors' quarters damp and cold."

"You two better get below," shouted a burly sailor. The wind made a loud hum through the rigging, and the sails flapped furiously.

Luke tugged at the heavy canvas piled near the cages. "We need to cover the animals," he shouted over the wind.

The sailor helped them lash the cover over the

cages. "Now get yourselves below," he said. "And stay there."

"Yes, sir," Luke said meekly.

The sailor grinned widely. "No need to call me sir. But you do as I say anyway. We've got enough to do without rescuing you two."

Luke looked back as he tugged open the door and slipped into the safety of the first-class passageway. In spite of the wind and cold, some sailors crawled over the rigging, furling the sails before the storm. Others had latched wooden shutters across the skylights, and these, too, were covered with canvas, making it dark below. Uncle Eli had lit two whale oil lamps in the saloon and hung them securely from hooks on the rafters. They swayed wildly with each roll of the ship and cast strange shadows on the mirrored walls. "There you are," he said, sounding relieved. "The storm came up faster than I thought."

"And just look at you two," Colleen said. "You get out of those wet things and into something dry this minute."

The boys were only too happy to obey. They groped their way to their cabin and changed quickly. Toby groaned and sprawled on his bunk, desperately hugging a tin bowl.

Luke gave his friend a sympathetic pat. Toby's skin was almost pasty colored, and sweat beaded on his forehead.

"Uncle Eli says it helps to eat," Luke said. "Try some of these crackers."

Toby moaned. "I can't."

Luke sighed and climbed into his own bunk. His own stomach was doing strange things as the ship lifted, then slammed down against the waves.

"What if the ship sinks and we are trapped in here?" Toby called over the noise of the storm.

"It won't," Luke said sharply, trying to convince himself. "Captain Andrews knows what he's doing. Uncle Eli said he was the captain of a whaling ship."

"I'm just glad Mama's not here," Toby gasped.

Luke had to hold the sides of his bunk to keep from being tossed out. On each roll of the ship their bags, books, and everything else not packed away slid across the room and then back again. With every minute the storm seemed to grow worse. Even inside the sturdy cabin section Luke could hear the pounding rain on the shuttered skylights and the howling wind. The ship rolled and creaked, and with every resounding thump as she hit the waves Luke feared she would break apart. He bit his lip to keep from crying out in fear.

Finally there was a quick knock on the door. It opened a crack, and Luke saw the cabin boy swaying in the faint light of a lantern. "Miss Colleen sent me to see if you were all right and ask if you were hungry," he said, raising his voice over the storm. "Weather's too wild to cook supper, but I could bring you some bread and cheese."

Luke leaned up on one elbow. "We're not hungry," he said. "We're both sick."

The cabin boy nodded. "Aye, me, too. At least you're not as bad off as the passengers between decks. I've never seen anything like it. People are heaving; luggage is flying about." He held his nose. "Stinks awful down there. Even if the sea doesn't make you sick, the smell will." The boy hesitated for a second at the door. "If you're all right, I'd better get back to the captain," he added.

"We'll be all right," Toby said weakly.

Jim opened the door. Then he looked back with a crooked grin. "Hooray for a delightful day at sea. Only one hundred and nine to go."

Despite their misery, Luke and Toby couldn't help laughing.

FIVE

Practical Jokes

The storm lasted two more long, miserable days before it stopped as quickly as it had started. The sun came out and dried the swollen boards, the sails were unfurled, and life at sea truly began. Luggage was safely stowed away, and the tween decks cleaned. Unlike many ships, where the tween decks area was completely closed in, the *Eagle* had air vents, installed by Uncle Eli. Even so, a faint unpleasant odor lingered even after scrubbing. Most of the men preferred to spend their days on deck.

Mr. Browning stopped other passengers on the deck to complain loudly about everything. His room was too small; he didn't like the food; the smell was awful. The list of complaints went on and on. Finally Mr. Appleby, who had volunteered to share a room with this disagreeable man, had heard enough.

"This is a fine ship," he said loyally. "Everyone else is pleased. It's not the captain's fault that we ran into a storm. Mr. Eli Reed was kind enough to let you come on the ship at the last minute. I'm the one who should complain. I offered to share my own small space, and instead of gratitude now I must listen to grumbling all day."

Several other passengers cheered Mr. Appleby's speech. Mr. Browning gave him a look shot through with daggers. With a loud *humpf*, he went back to his room.

"It will be a bit uncomfortable sharing a room with that fellow after that," Uncle Eli said.

Mr. Appleby shook his head. "If I'm lucky, maybe Mr. Browning won't speak to me the rest of the trip."

Toby and Luke laughed over the argument while they cared for the chickens and goats. The morning after the storm they had nervously untied the canvas covers over the cages, expecting the worst. The animals, however, had survived in good shape. As the boys cleaned the cages and spread fresh straw, Toby poked Luke. "Look at George. He's thinking about a good chicken dinner."

The chickens clucked nervously as George slunk around their cages. "Shoo, George," Toby said. "If anyone around here gets a chicken dinner, it's going to be me and not you."

George stalked away, his tail twitching. He ran lightly up the stairs to the poop deck, where the captain was shouting orders to his men.

"I don't think the captain ever sleeps," Luke said.

"He sure has a soft spot for that cat," Toby remarked as the captain bent down, picked up George, and put him on his shoulder. The cat curled around the captain's neck and rubbed against his ear as though he were whispering orders.

Colleen came on deck to milk the goats. They gave enough milk to use for cooking, and Colleen saw to it that the boys got at least a small cupful every day. "I'm going to give some of this milk to Jim," she said as the cabin boy hurried by with a stack of new canvas for the sailmaker. "He's much too thin," she declared. Luke thought it was no wonder the boy was so thin. Every time Luke saw him he was doing a chore for someone. Cabin boy seemed to be the lowest position on the ship. From early morning until late at night the boy carried messages, served food, and helped clean the galley and the pantry.

The ship cut through the water so smoothly that hardly anyone was still sick, although Mr. Appleby often looked pale when he gave them their lessons. Mr. Appleby was a strict taskmaster when it came to their studies, but Luke and Toby liked him. At the end of each lesson he allowed them to sit on deck while he read aloud from the supply of books Uncle Eli had brought with him. The first book he'd chosen was *Oliver Twist* by Charles Dickens. So well did he read that usually a small crowd gathered around to listen.

The members of the Boston Mining Company spent much of their time on deck, reading or playing cards, chess, or checkers. In the close quarters of the ship Luke and Toby soon got to know most of the men. They were especially fond of Judge Myer and Mr. Beardsly.

"Are you going to dig for gold?" Luke asked Judge Myer one day.

"I might try my hand at it," the judge replied. "But the truth is, I thought with all these new mining claims there would be a need for lawyers and courts. There's talk about making California a state," he added. "Seems like it might be pretty exciting to be a part of that."

"I figure with so many new people there will be a need for carpenters," Mr. Beardsly said in his soft voice. He waved his arm at the other passengers. "Most of them dream of getting rich. I just want some adventure."

An argument between two passengers interrupted the conversation. Each had a guidebook to the goldfields and believed that his was correct and the other's false. A crowd gathered around, listening to the heated discussion. Finally Uncle Eli broke it up. "I don't believe either one of those authors has ever been to California," he said. "You might as well toss both books overboard."

As the days passed, everyone looked for ways to break the boredom. Often the most exciting event was a checkers game. Sometimes ten men would be gathered around watching the opponents. When Luke took out his paints, a large crowd was always ready to give helpful advice.

One person who never seemed bored was Mr. Colville. He was a quiet young man who had two passions, reading and fishing. Every morning found him on the poop deck directly over the first-class cabins. With his fishing line dangling over the rail he leaned back in his chair and read. Day after day he spent in this fashion, seldom catching anything but completely content.

One day Mr. Beardsly pulled Luke and Toby aside. "Some of the fellows have been talking," he said with a sly smile. "It's a shame how Mr. Colville waits so patiently for a good catch. Some of us have it in mind to help him out."

"How would you do that?" Luke asked.

"We have a plan," was all Mr. Beardsly answered. "But we need some help from you two."

"What can we do?" Toby asked.

Quickly Mr. Beardsly outlined his plan. The boys were to go to the opposite side of the main deck, out of sight from Mr. Colville's usual place. Then they were to create some kind of disturbance, something interesting enough to make even Mr. Colville rush to see.

"What can we do?" Luke asked as they took their place.

"I have an idea," Toby said. Cupping his hands, he shouted loudly, "Sharks! Sharks! Look at all the sharks in the water."

It worked only too well. Except those in on the plan, nearly everyone on board came running and clustered along the rail. Mr. Colville pushed his way to the front and peered into the dark water. "Where?" he shouted. "How many?"

One day in Boston Harbor Luke had seen a shark that some fishermen had harpooned. "Ten, twenty," he yelled. "Monstrous big things. Teeth this big." He held his hands wide apart.

The men stared out over the water for several minutes. Then one by one they drifted away.

"Are you sure you saw them?" Mr. Colville asked.

Toby nodded seriously. "They were there. I guess they're gone now."

With a disappointed look Mr. Colville went back to his place. When he picked up his pole, however, he suddenly shouted, "I've hooked something. Something big."

"Maybe it's one of those sharks," said Mr. Beardsly, cheering him on.

"I've heard shark meat is good to eat," shouted another man.

"It's putting up a ferocious fight," Mr. Colville grunted.

By now nearly everyone on the ship had heard of the joke and had come to watch. Mr. Colville let out his line, allowing the "shark" to tire itself out. Bit by bit he reeled in the line. "Ought to catch a glimpse of it pretty soon," he said, his face glistening with sweat.

Mr. Beardsly and several others jumped into action. "We'll help you pull it in," they shouted gaily. "Stand back, everyone. Don't want to get caught by those snapping teeth."

Mr. Colville looked alarmed, but he refused all offers of help until finally he hauled the catch over the rail and down on the deck. Everyone on the ship roared with laughter at the porcelain chamber pot carefully tied to the end of the line.

Mr. Colville looked angry. Then he laughed, too. "You got me good, boys. But from now on you'll have to watch your step. You'll never know when I'll get my revenge."

One afternoon Colleen dispatched three chickens. Two she gave to the cook to prepare for the passengers and crew. The third she made into a delicious stew for the first-class passengers, followed by a dessert called dandy funk made with broken pieces of dry biscuits baked with molasses.

"Colleen, you are a wonder," Uncle Eli said, pushing himself away from the table. "I'll wager there isn't another ship on the high seas serving a better meal tonight."

"Colleen will make somebody a fine wife," Mr. Beardsly said.

Colleen blushed. "You gentlemen are embarrassing me with all that flattery."

Luke and Toby left the adults to their talk and went up on deck. It was a warm night, and the moon shone nearly as bright as day. Somebody was playing a fiddle, and someone else brought out a flute and a tambourine. After a time Mr. Beardsly came on deck and started to sing in a surprisingly good voice, and several others joined in.

Toby and Luke leaned back against the goat pens, listening to the music. The judge danced with Colleen. Then Uncle Eli asked her to dance. He swirled her around and around, while Colleen smiled up at him. Toby poked Luke in the side with his elbow. "Colleen likes your uncle."

"Uncle Eli?" Luke asked. "He's too old for Colleen."

Jim walked by with an armload of canvas for the sailmaker. He stood beside Luke and Toby, watching the dancers. "He's not that old," he remarked. "Looks to me like he's sweet on her, too."

Luke stared at Uncle Eli and Colleen. They did seem to be enjoying each other's company. Mr. Beardsly and the judge stood side by side, waiting their turn to dance with Colleen, but she did not seem to notice.

"I have to get back to work," Jim said, sounding unhappy.

"Sometime when you're off work, come to our cabin. We can play checkers or something," Luke said.

Jim shrugged. "Captain wouldn't like me visiting with the passengers."

"Captain wouldn't have to know," Toby said. "He must sleep sometime."

"Being a cabin boy is a rough job. Why would you want to do it?" Luke asked.

"I need to get to California," Jim said. "I thought about trying to stow away. But this way I get paid a little, so I won't be broke when I get there."

"Hey, Jim," said the captain in his booming voice, "fetch me a cup of tea. And be quick about it."

"Yes, sir," Jim called.

"Why do you want to go to California so much?" Toby asked as Jim started to leave. "Are you going to search for gold?"

"In a way," Jim said. He lowered his voice. "I may own a gold mine already."

Luke and Toby stared at him in surprise.

"I'll try to come to your room later and explain," Jim said.

Just then Captain Andrews came close enough to give him a hard cuff across his shoulders. "I said be quick," the captain growled.

"Yes, sir. Sorry." Jim hurried away.

Luke heard a faint rustle and looked behind him. Mr. Browning stepped out of the shadows. He nodded briefly as he passed. Since Mr. Appleby's scolding he seemed to be making an effort to be friendlier. He spoke to several passengers and then stood for several minutes talking with Mr. Levering, the first mate. They fell silent as the boys walked by, and Mr. Levering gave them a cold stare.

SIX

Jim's Story

"I don't like Mr. Levering at all," Toby remarked as they returned to their quarters.

Luke nodded. "I heard Uncle Eli say the man who was supposed to be first mate broke his leg and couldn't go. Captain Andrews didn't like Mr. Levering either, but he had his first mate's papers, and there wasn't time to look for another."

They walked back to their cabin, and Luke looked at the pile of books on the small desk. "I guess we should work on our studies," he said.

Toby nodded and picked up a thick book he was reading. Luke sighed, looking at his own easy primer. Watching the members of the Boston Mining Company as they filled their long hours aboard ship with reading or discussing books made him realize how important schooling was. Now it seemed as if he would never catch up.

The boys set to work. An hour or so later there was a tap on the door. It was Jim. "The captain finally went to bed," he said.

Toby set a lamp on the floor, and the three of them sat around it.

"Now," Luke said, "tell us what you meant about owning a gold mine."

Jim took a deep breath. "Last year my father went to California. He left me with our landlords, the Pembrooks—"

"What about your mother?" Toby asked.

"She died when I was a baby. Anyway, the Pembrooks seemed nice enough, and at first everything was fine. Then months went by and we didn't hear a word from my father. Mrs. Pembrook started complaining that it was costing too much to feed me and they had used up all the money Father had left for my care."

"Did they throw you out on the street?" Luke asked.

"No," Jim answered. "Because finally a letter

came. Father said he had found gold and wanted me to join him. He sent money for a ticket." Jim's voice broke, and the boys waited a minute before he could continue. "The letter took three months to arrive.

"The Pembrooks were happy to get rid of me, but right after I got the letter a man came to the house. He told the Pembrooks that my father was dead. He'd found Father's body at his camp and buried him.

"But before he left, the man talked to me alone. He told me that Father had still been alive when he got to the camp. He said that before he died, my father told the man that he didn't trust the Pembrooks. He said he'd left the deed to a gold mine and the map that said how to get there in a safe place. And he had given me a message telling me how I could find them. The man said that Father made him promise that he would bring me a box of his things."

"So what was in the box?" Toby asked.

"My father's pocket watch, a portrait of my mother, and a book."

"That was all?" Luke sounded disappointed.

Jim nodded. "I thought the message must be somewhere in that box, but I couldn't find anything. Mr. Pembrook took the watch to pay for my keep. Then the Pembrooks said I could stay, but only if I wanted to be Mrs. Pembrook's servant and sleep in the barn."

"So that's when you decided to go to California," Luke said.

Jim nodded. "But the Pembrooks took the money for my ticket, too. They wouldn't believe me when I said I knew nothing about my father's gold mine. I think they suspected my father had given me a secret message. The last few days they kept watching me, and I thought they had searched my room. Luckily I had hidden the box under a loose board in the wardrobe." Jim sighed. "Then I saw the sign advertising for a cabin boy on the *Eagle*. It seemed like the perfect way to escape the Pembrooks. I changed my appearance as much as I could and left that day. All the way to the ship I thought I was being followed. I guess I was just imagining that."

"What will you do when you reach California?" Luke asked.

"Maybe I can get a job," Jim said. "Then I'll look

for someone who knew my father," he added hope-
fully.

"We should tell Uncle Eli. I'll bet he could help
you."

Jim shook his head. "I don't want anyone else to
know. There is a reason, but I can't say what it is.
I promise I'll tell you when we get to California.
Please don't tell anyone else."

Luke and Toby reluctantly agreed to keep Jim's
secret.

It was a hot, sticky night. Luke got up before
dawn and went on deck, hoping to find some
cooler air. The first watch was just getting ready
to go to work. The sailors sipped their coffee in tin
cups while Mr. Levering drank his from one made
of china. When he finished, he handed his cup to
Jim to wash and put away so it wouldn't get broken. "Turn to, forward, and wash down decks," he
called.

Instantly the sailors put down their own cups
and rolled up their trouser legs. Some of them
gathered up the coils of rope that lay about. The
others scrubbed the deck with a mixture of salt
water and sand. Luke knew this not only kept the

planks clean but also made them swell to keep out leaks below. Then the decks were swabbed dry while sailors scurried over the rigging, tightening the ropes.

Captain Andrews came up for a morning sighting through the sextant. Uncle Eli had explained that each day the ship's speed, position, and weather were written down in the captain's logbook.

The smell of cooking ham brought a growl to Luke's stomach, and he realized it was already eight o'clock. The sailors were allowed time for their breakfasts while a new bunch came on deck.

After breakfast Mr. Appleby came to their cabin, and for the rest of the day the boys were busy with their lessons. That evening they went on deck to care for the animals. Just as they were about to go back inside, they heard a hiss. It was Mr. Colville. "I've thought of my revenge," he whispered. "I need your help."

He pointed silently to the huge bucket of seawater he had suspended over the door to the first-class cabins. "Any minute now Mr. Beardsly will be coming through the door. I need one of you to watch and tell me when."

Smiling, Luke nodded. "But how do you know he's coming?"

Mr. Colville chuckled gleefully. "Because he found a note under his door this morning. He thinks it was from a certain young lady on board asking him to meet her on deck at nine o'clock."

Toby laughed. "Poor Mr. Beardsly."

"Fair is fair," said Mr. Colville. "It's no worse than fishing for a chamber pot."

"I'll go," Luke said. Leaving Toby with Mr. Colville, he slipped inside the passageway and hid in a doorway, watching for Mr. Beardsly. The word had traveled around the ship that Mr. Colville was at last to get his revenge. Several other men, with winks at Luke, went up on deck to watch the fun.

Sure enough, just before nine o'clock Mr. Beardsly left his room. He was wearing his finest suit of clothes, and his beard was neatly trimmed.

Luke jumped up and raced to the doorway ahead of him. "You're in a big hurry," Mr. Beardsly said good-naturedly.

"I left my book on deck," Luke called back. He burst through the door to the deck. "He's coming," he whispered hoarsely.

Grinning with excitement, Mr. Colville held the

ropes, but seconds ticked by, and the door did not open. "Where is he?" Mr. Colville asked.

"Maybe he went back to his room for something," answered Luke, equally puzzled. "He was right behind me."

"Shh," someone whispered. Luke held his breath as the door handle turned and the door opened. A man stepped on deck.

"Wait," called Luke. "It's Captain Andrews." His voice trailed off in dismay as five gallons of cold seawater splashed over the captain's portly figure.

"What is this?" Captain Andrews spluttered.

Poor Mr. Colville was beside himself. "I'm sorry," he mumbled over and over. He tore off his own shirt and mopped at the captain, trying to dry him off.

Captain Andrews pushed Mr. Colville out of the way. "Explain yourself, sir," he roared.

Mr. Colville was too horrified to answer. The other passengers were either standing in wide-eyed shock or hiding loud snickers behind their hands. Mr. Beardsly poked his head out of the door. He laughed out loud when he realized what had happened. "I believe that was meant for me,

Captain," he explained between loud guffaws. "I stopped to talk to Mr. Lane." He looked at Luke and laughed again. "So that's why you were in such a hurry."

Mr. Colville was still trying to dry the captain. "Stop," the captain roared. "There will be no more horseplay aboard my ship. Is that understood?"

"Yes, sir," Mr. Colville replied meekly.

All the next day the story was told over and over, each time growing as stories tend to do. Everyone enjoyed it immensely, except for Mr. Colville. He had retreated once more behind his books and his fishing pole and did not speak to anyone all day.

SEVEN

Becalmed

Jim came to the boys' room several nights later. At Toby's request he brought his father's box. It was a plain, smooth, wooden box, and even though they examined it closely, it did not reveal any clues.

Next they picked up the small silver frame and stared at the portrait of Jim's mother. "She was pretty," Luke said. "You look like her a little."

"I don't remember her," Jim said, looking at the picture. His eyes looked sad. "I took it out of the frame and checked carefully," he said. "Nothing." He started to put it back in the box, but Toby stopped him. "What's that on the bottom?"

"I saw that," Jim said, "but it doesn't make sense. I think it must be the silversmith's mark."

Luke peered at the markings. "A-three," he read aloud.

"It's too new to be the silversmith's mark, and it looks like it was just scratched on. Maybe it's a clue of some kind," Toby said.

Jim looked doubtful.

"Do you know someone whose name starts with A?" Luke asked.

Jim shook his head. "I don't think so."

"It might be a code for a message," Toby said thoughtfully. "You know, "A-three, B-four. Have you seen anything with a lot of numbers?"

Jim shook his head. "Nothing."

"What about the book?" Luke asked. "You said there was a book."

"It's in my room," Jim answered. "I've looked all through it. There's nothing written anywhere."

"Next time you come, bring it anyway," Toby said. "Maybe if we all look at it, we'll see something."

"I'd better go before the captain misses me," Jim said. He picked up the box and swung the door open, nearly knocking down Mr. Browning, who was right outside.

"Watch where you're going," Mr. Browning bellowed.

"Sorry, sir," Jim mumbled.

"Now, Mr. Browning, it was an accident plain and simple," said Mr. Appleby. He squeezed past Mr. Browning in the narrow passageway.

"Members of the crew should not be spending time with the passengers," Mr. Browning said. "It's against the rules."

"He just brought us some tea," Luke said.

Mr. Appleby patted Jim's back. "Go along about your business, boy," he said kindly.

"He's a hardworking lad. I don't think there is any harm in his having a bit of conversation with Luke and Toby," Mr. Appleby said to Mr. Browning when Jim was out of hearing distance. Luke gave him a grateful look.

"These boys shouldn't be spending time with the likes of that," Mr. Browning said stubbornly. "I have half a notion to report him to the captain." He abruptly turned away, then stuck his head back in the door. "What's that boy's name, anyway?"

Luke was too startled to answer, but Toby said

smoothly, "I think I heard the captain call him Jim."

"I hope Mr. Browning doesn't make trouble for Jim," Luke said when Mr. Browning was gone.

"I wouldn't worry about him," said Mr. Appleby. "Some people just aren't happy unless they have something to complain about. I suspect Captain Andrews is aware of Mr. Browning's nature. I of course will speak up for the lad if there is trouble."

After thanking Mr. Appleby, the boys went to bed. It was difficult to sleep. The cabin was stuffy and warm, and the bedclothes felt damp. When they awoke the next morning, the heat was almost unbearable. They had been traveling for nearly a month, and the weather had been getting warmer every day. Now waves of heat radiated from the passenger quarters, making it impossible to stay below for more than a few minutes. Passengers and crew alike spent all their time on the decks. With Jim's help the boys had erected a canvas cover to keep the animals from the worst of the sun. Luke sat under the tarp by the pens trying to paint. Toby sat nearby, listlessly reading a book or staring out at the smooth, endless ocean.

It stayed hot that night and for the following days. In the daytime passengers stretched extra pieces of canvas over the deck to shade themselves from the burning sun. At night the deck was crowded with people sleeping in every corner. As if the unbearable heat were not enough, there was no wind to move the ship along. For weeks now they had skimmed across the ocean ahead of schedule. Now the *Eagle* bobbed silently, waiting for a breath of air to help them on their way. Even worse, the water stored in wooden barrels all these weeks was slimy and warm and had to be rationed. The men grumbled and complained. Instead of the good-natured teasing of a few weeks ago, tempers flared.

Only two things happened to break the monotony. First Mr. Colville's fishing finally paid off with the catch of four huge fish, enough to feed everyone on board. This made Mr. Colville something of a hero for the day, which pleased him greatly. The second thing was that the ship crossed the equator.

It was the custom to have some sort of festivity for the occasion. Captain Andrews ordered the passengers to gather on the main deck right after supper. They milled about, not sure what to expect.

"What's going to happen?" Luke asked.

"I don't know," Uncle Eli answered.

"We have a special visitor," Captain Andrews announced. "Please welcome King Neptune and his wife."

EIGHT

Neptune's Visit

Everyone laughed and clapped as the visitors climbed up a rope ladder and over the rail. Queen Neptune, in a gown and straw hat, looked suspiciously like the sailor with the bad teeth. King Neptune wore long, flowing robes, and his beard was made of rope.

"Ho, Your Majesty," Captain Andrews said in a hearty voice. "We are honored to have you aboard our humble ship."

"I've come to give my blessing to those passing the line for the first time," King Neptune said in a gruff voice.

"The ship is all yours," Captain Andrews said.

King Neptune inspected the ship. He asked

about the food and, when the passengers declared Colleen's cooking fit for a king, insisted on eating a biscuit to test it for himself. "This is delicious," he announced. "Why don't you cook like this?" he asked his wife.

"Did you ever try to light a stove under the sea?" asked Queen Neptune. The crowd laughed, and Toby grinned at Luke. "This is fun."

Luke nodded. "I think today is the first time I ever saw Captain Andrews smile."

"He does seem almost human," Toby said.

Mr. Browning squeezed in beside Luke. "I've been meaning to talk to you. That night when the cabin boy bumped into me, I lost my temper. I do apologize."

Taken by surprise, Luke and Toby exchanged a quick look. "That's all right," Luke mumbled.

"I'm afraid sometimes my nature is a bit crusty," said Mr. Browning. "It's only that I'm so worried about my brother all the time."

Luke nodded. "I understand."

Mr. Browning looked around. "Actually this is a wonderful ship. I understand your uncle is planning to sell everything in the hold when he gets to California. That's quite an investment. Your uncle must be a very rich man."

Luke nodded, suddenly uncomfortable with the conversation. "I see Mr. Appleby," he said, excusing himself. "We need to ask him about our lessons."

A look of annoyance passed over Mr. Browning's face. "Of course," he said abruptly.

Luke and Toby pushed their way through the crowd until they reached the tutor. "I saw you talking to Mr. Browning," said Mr. Appleby. "I suppose he's complaining again."

Luke shrugged. "He was talking about Jim. He actually apologized."

The tutor raised his eyebrows in surprise.

King Neptune and his wife sang a song and entertained with jokes. Luke and Toby watched the show with Mr. Appleby. "Are you going to teach school in California?" Toby asked.

"I'm going to find gold," the tutor said. "Your uncle has been kind, but schoolteachers get paid only a pittance." Mr. Appleby sounded bitter.

Luke didn't know how to answer, but the tutor went on in a calmer voice. "I have been thinking about Jim. Perhaps we should include him in our lessons. He's an interesting boy. He seems fairly well spoken for a cabin boy. Is this his first time at sea?" he asked.

Luke nodded. "He's an orphan."

"That explains it then," Mr. Appleby said. "Perhaps his parents gave him some schooling. How did they die?"

"His mother died when he was a baby," Luke said. "His father died not long ago."

"Poor boy," said Mr. Appleby. "Was there no inheritance at all?"

"No," Luke answered.

"Everyone sure is curious tonight," Toby whispered to Luke.

Mr. Appleby seemed to have lost interest. "Look," he said with a laugh. Captain Andrews escorted King Neptune and his wife to a throne made of several crates piled on top of one another.

"Everyone who has not passed over the equator before, come down in front and sit," said Captain Andrews. "King Neptune has a few words to say to you."

That was nearly all the passengers. Luke and Toby squeezed in front so they could see. The canvas deck covers over their heads flapped as a cooling breeze came up. Some of the sailors gathered behind the passengers; others scrambled up into the rigging.

Colleen was sitting next to Uncle Eli. She smiled when she saw Luke. He waved back happily.

"I am the king of the sea," roared King Neptune.

Mrs. Neptune batted her eyelashes. Her face was covered with a fluttering fan. "Oh yes, dear, everyone knows that."

"Do you believe that?" he asked the passengers.

"Yes, we believe that," answered the crowd.

"I cause the wind and the rain," said Neptune, waving his arms wildly. "Do you believe?"

"We believe," shouted the passengers. No sooner had they spoken than the canvas dropped and bucket after bucket of water splashed down on the unsuspecting audience.

The sailors laughed as they swung down from the rigging with their empty buckets. "You now have my permission to sail the seven seas," King Neptune shouted over the passengers' laughing and sputtering. Luke and Toby were drenched, but the damp clothing made them feel cooler.

"This calls for a celebration," said Mr. Lane. He brought out his fiddle, and Neptune and his wife did a lively dance about the deck. Luke and Toby clapped their hands in time to the music. Then, as if at Neptune's command, a steady breeze came up. While the passengers cheered, the crew scrambled to turn the sails to catch the wind.

"If we can keep this wind, we'll be at our first port before long," Uncle Eli told the boys.

Judge Myer grabbed Colleen and twirled her about the deck. Her hair had come undone because of the water, and she was laughing as she danced by. "My turn next," called Mr. Beardsly.

"I think it's my turn," Uncle Eli said. He whirled Colleen away while the two men watched with long faces.

Luke spied Jim standing in the shadows watching the merriment and clapping his hands to the music. "Captain Andrews gave me the whole day off," Jim said. He looked around nervously. "I hope Mr. Browning doesn't see me talking to you and cause trouble."

"Mr. Browning apologized for that. And Uncle Eli wouldn't let you get into trouble just for talking to us anyway," Luke told him.

Jim still looked uncomfortable, so Luke and Toby

took him to their favorite spot, the hidden corner by the animal cages. Jim poked his fingers into the goats' cages and petted the smallest one.

"Toby and I named that one Maggie," Luke said. "Be careful. She likes to eat your clothes."

Maggie nibbled at Jim's shirt. He laughed and pulled his arm away. As he did, he knocked over a drawing pad Luke had left nearby. Jim picked it up and looked at the sketches inside.

"These are great," Jim said. "You're a wonderful artist."

Luke sighed, looking out over the night sea. "I've been trying to draw the ocean, but it's so hard, like the prairie. Miles and miles of sameness. Yet when you really look, you see that it is constantly changing. I wish it were possible to make moving pictures."

Toby and Jim laughed. "Moving pictures. What a silly idea!" Jim said.

They talked until they could not stay awake any longer. Finally Jim said a reluctant good-night. "Captain will expect me to work twice as hard tomorrow to make up for today," he said.

Luke and Toby returned to their cabin, but they

had been there only a few minutes when there was a soft tap at the door. Jim was holding the box from his father.

"Would you hide this for me?" he asked. "I know it's silly, but I think someone was in my room. This morning I pulled the covers up neatly on my bed, but when I got back tonight they were wrinkled as though someone had sat on them."

"And you think they were looking for this?" Luke said, taking the box.

Jim shrugged. "Like I said, it's probably nothing. But I can't think of any other reason someone would be interested in a cabin boy's room. You wanted to look at the book anyway."

"If that was what they were searching for, why didn't they find it?" Luke asked.

"I had all that lovely time off yesterday, and I was going to sit in the pantry and read. Then Colleen came in, and we talked. She told me about the voyage from Ireland and how kind your uncle was to the Irish people who came to Boston. That's when they called for everyone who hadn't crossed the equator to come on deck, and I left the book in the pantry."

Toby opened the box and looked at the book. "*Jane Eyre*," he read. He opened to the first page. " 'To my sweet Louisa,' " he read. "I thought you said your father sent the book to you."

Jim hesitated before answering. "Louisa was my mother. Maybe that's why father wanted me to have it."

It sounded true. Yet Jim looked away, and Luke had the feeling that there was something he wasn't telling.

Toby gave Jim a thoughtful stare. "Have you told anyone else about the gold mine?"

"No one."

"How about your plans to get to California on this ship?" Toby asked.

Jim looked stricken. "The Pembrooks have a daughter named Clara. I told her. I thought she was my friend."

After Jim left, Toby looked thoughtful. "Jim lied to us," he said.

Seeing Luke's startled look, he went on. "This book couldn't have belonged to his mother."

"Why not?" Luke asked.

Toby pointed to the publication date on the first page.

"Eighteen forty-seven," Luke read.

"This is 1850. We know Jim's mother died when he was a baby. If this really was his mother's book, then Jim would have to be three years old," Toby said.

"Why would he lie?" Luke asked.

"That's what I'd like to know," Toby answered.

NINE

————— ◆ —————

Secrets

Luke, unable to sleep, tossed and turned on the narrow bunk. Why had Jim lied to them? Was it possible the whole story about the gold mine wasn't true? Luke remembered the tears in Jim's eyes when he told them about his father's death. Surely that part was real. He thought about Jim's dying father. If he'd known he was dying, wouldn't he at least have written his son's name somewhere in the box's contents, hoping it might reach him? Slowly Luke sat up. Jim's father *had* written something. "To my sweet Louisa." That was what he'd written as he was dying in California.

"Toby, are you awake?" Luke called down.

"No" came Toby's sleepy reply.

Luke jumped off his bunk and shook his friend. "Jim is a girl," he said loudly.

Toby sat up and rubbed his eyes. "What?"

"I think I know Jim's secret. He's a girl, and her name is Louisa."

Toby laughed. "That must have been some dream you were just having."

"No," Luke said. "Listen." Carefully he explained his reasons, including how closely the portrait of "his" mother resembled "Jim."

Toby was silent when he finished. Then slowly he nodded. "I just thought of something else. Remember when Jim told us about getting ready to be a cabin boy? He said he tried to change his appearance as much as possible." He snapped his fingers. "That might be the secret he promised to tell us when we reached California."

"Now what do we do?" Luke asked.

Toby hesitated. "We're not even sure we are right. We can't just accuse him of being a girl. If we are wrong he'd be really upset."

"So what should we do?" Luke asked.

"Maybe just wait and see what happens," Toby said. "Until he tells us something different, he'll stay Jim. Tomorrow I'm going to look at every page in that book for some sort of message. But right now I am going back to sleep."

Luke climbed back into bed. In less than a minute he heard Toby's gentle breathing. But it was a long time before he himself fell asleep.

The next morning a brisk breeze swept the *Eagle* along at a good pace. "We are fortunate," Uncle Eli said when Luke came on deck after breakfast. "Sometimes ships are becalmed for weeks in these waters."

Luke looked for Jim—or Louisa, he reminded himself—but Captain Andrews kept him busy, and there was no chance to talk. He watched the cabin boy scurrying around the ship doing errands. There was no sign of a girl under the ragged clothes and dirty face, but Luke was sure he was right.

Even though the breeze stayed with them for the next few days, the passengers grumbled. Mr. Browning, of course, grumbled the loudest of all. The fresh fruits and vegetables had been gone for weeks. Although Colleen baked several pies using dried apples and shared the few remaining jars of jams and jellies, their diet consisted of mostly salt pork, beans, and biscuits. It was the water that caused the most grumbling, however. Warm and slimy from storage in wooden barrels, it could be made drinkable only with a few drops of vinegar and molasses. Even then most people held their noses to drink.

There was a brief break in the monotony one morning when Judge Myer and Mr. Beardsly spotted several albatrosses. The two men had become fast friends, perhaps united in their unhappiness that Colleen spent almost all her free time with Uncle Eli.

"We must be near land," Mr. Beardsly said, scanning the horizon.

"Not necessarily," said the judge. "Albatrosses sometimes live on the ocean for months. They drink seawater and even sleep floating on the seas."

"Look how big they are!" Luke exclaimed as one of the giant birds flew off.

"They can have wingspreads of up to eleven feet," the judge remarked.

Even Jim took a minute to watch. "I'm sorry I haven't had time to come to your cabin," he said. "The captain keeps me so busy, and sometimes I help Colleen in the kitchen. I've seen you watching me sometimes," he added. "Is something wrong?"

Luke, embarrassed, shook his head. "No," he said quickly. "I was just thinking I might like to paint a picture of you."

A slight smile crossed Jim's face. "Let's wait until we get to California," he said.

When Jim was gone, Luke watched the men amusing themselves by throwing bits of hard biscuit for the birds to catch with their strong, hooked beaks. But after a time even that grew boring. As the albatrosses followed them for several days, the men went back to their bickering and quarreling.

One morning Luke was sitting on deck drawing the sailors busy in the rigging with the daily chore of tightening the ropes. Captain Andrews stood nearby, with George curled peacefully around his neck. Suddenly a large gray shape leaped from the water and dived back in with a graceful arc. "What was that?" Luke asked.

"A dolphin," Captain Andrews said. "Sometimes a whole school will follow a ship."

A blunt, friendly face popped out of the water

quite near the *Eagle*. The dolphin made a curious clicking noise.

Luke sketched furiously, trying to capture the creature before it disappeared. Several passengers gathered around to watch the drawing take shape.

Suddenly Toby came on deck clutching a piece of paper and motioning for Luke to follow him. Luke put away his drawing materials and hurried to the goat pens. On the way he passed Jim carrying a bucket of slops, which he emptied over the rail to the ocean below.

"Toby has found something," he whispered. "Can you get away?"

Jim glanced at the captain, whose back was turned, and nodded.

They sat in the corner where they were hidden from view. "I kept thinking about that clue, you know, A-three?" When Jim and Luke nodded, Toby continued. "I got to thinking maybe it was something to do with the page numbers, so I was checking them. Then I noticed a dot under a letter on one page. There was one on the next page and the page after that. At any rate I wrote down all the letters in the book that had dots."

Jim held the copy of *Jane Eyre* and peered where Toby pointed on a page. Luke looked over his shoulder. There it was: a faint dot under the letter G.

"So what does it say?" he asked.

Toby looked determined. "I don't know yet. But I'm sure it means something. Look."

He handed them a paper:

GHDUGDXJKWHUVLFNGHHGWRJROGLVD
WVDFUDPHQWRSRVWRIILFHFRPHDWRQFH

Jim's hopeful face fell. "That's it?" he asked. "This doesn't make any sense."

"I'm sure it's a message," Toby said. "I just need time to think about it."

Mr. Browning suddenly peered around the goat pen. "Why so excited?" he asked. Toby quickly folded the paper.

"It's just a game we are playing," Luke said.

Suddenly a glad cry came up from the mast: "*Land ho!*" Mr. Browning hurried away without another word.

"Do you think he saw the message?" Jim asked.

"Even if he did, he couldn't make any sense out of it," Toby told him.

"I have to go before the captain starts looking for me," Jim said.

They watched as he headed back to his chores. "He sure doesn't act like a girl," Toby said.

"I know I'm right," Luke said.

Toby shrugged. "If it's true, he'll have to tell us sometime. Come on. Let's put this away and find out what's going on." They raced to their cabin, tucked the paper in the book, and put it safely away in the desk. Then they hurried to join the others on deck. Far in the distance the faint outline of a hill was visible.

Mr. Appleby rushed to the rail and squeezed in beside them. "I was below. What's all the excitement?" the tutor asked.

"Land," Luke said happily.

The tutor's face broke into smiles. "At last," he said joyfully.

TEN

Land Ho!

The good mood filled the whole ship. Petty differences were forgotten, and so many passengers lined up along the rail that it seemed the *Eagle* would tip. Luke and Toby squeezed in beside Judge Myer and Mr. Beardsly. Far off in the horizon was the misty shape of a hill. There was a circle of land just barely visible around it.

"That's Rio de Janeiro," someone said.

Colleen hurried on deck, wiping her hands on her apron. The men parted to let her get up to the rail. "Eli says we will have five days onshore," she said. "It will take that long to buy fruits and vegetables, get fresh water, and do any repairs before we get to the stormy seas around the cape."

"I hope you'll allow me to escort you on at least some of your sightseeing excursions," Judge Myer said gallantly.

"I would be pleased to take you to the botanical garden," said Mr. Beardsly. "I've heard it's lovely."

Uncle Eli slipped in beside Colleen and held his arm protectively around her waist. "I'm afraid Colleen is going to be busy while we're in port. She has agreed to be Mrs. Eli Reed. We're going to be married while we're in Rio."

Luke could not believe his ears. He looked at Toby, who smiled happily back. "That's great," both boys said together.

Mr. Beardsly and the judge looked crestfallen, but they quickly recovered, and the members of the Boston Mining Company gave the engaged couple a cheer.

"I think Miss Maisie had this in mind when she suggested I take Colleen," Uncle Eli said to Luke. "This voyage has given us time to know each other."

Colleen kissed Mr. Beardsly and the judge on their cheeks. "I hope you'll come to my wedding. You're both very special to me."

The passengers rushed away to pack. Some were dragging bags to the deck, hoping to be first onshore, when Captain Andrews raised his hand. "Hold on there," he shouted over the excitement. "It will take us a day to get into the harbor and put down anchor. And it takes another day to clear customs."

A groan went through the passengers. To be so close and still have to wait! It seemed nearly unbearable.

Ignoring the captain's warning, nearly all the passengers brought their baggage on deck. The men sat on stacks of their belongings, watching as the town came into view. The captain grumbled that there was hardly enough room for his crew to do their chores. Nevertheless the ship neatly turned and started into the harbor. Now Luke could see whitewashed houses and a riot of color from the flowers that dotted the hills. They passed under the cannon of Santa Cruz, a stone fortress guarding the harbor.

The bay was dotted with small islands, and several other tall-masted ships were at anchor near the docks. Toby pointed to one ship as they passed.

Unlike the *Eagle*, which Captain Andrews and his crew kept polished and neat, this ship looked as if it badly needed repair. Her sails were torn, and salt encrusted her rails. Four cannon filled her deck. Luke could just barely make out her name. "*Neptune's Surprise*," he read out loud.

The sound of church bells echoed across the bay. Luke and Toby returned to their room to pack a bag so that they, too, would be ready when the call came to go ashore. Toby opened the desk drawer and looked at Jim's book. "Wait a minute. Didn't I fold this paper when I put it in the drawer?"

The paper was in the book, but flat. A faint crease in the middle was still plain.

"You were in a hurry. Maybe you just thought you did."

Toby pointed to the lessons neatly stacked on the desk. "Mr. Appleby has been here."

The boys looked at each other. Finally Luke shook his head. "Mr. Appleby wouldn't look through our things."

"You're right," Toby said. Then he paused. "Mr. Appleby was there the day Jim bumped into Mr. Browning. He could have heard us talking. And you said he was asking all those questions about Jim."

Luke shook his head. "I think you just put the paper in there unfolded."

Toby shrugged. "Maybe." He tucked the book under his mattress. "Just in case," he said.

Luke tried to put the seed of suspicion out of his mind. He tried not to think about the bitter tone in Mr. Appleby's voice when he talked about how little money teachers made. He was going to California to look for gold, but surely he wouldn't steal that gold from someone else.

"I can hardly wait to get on land," Toby said as they walked up on deck. "I'll bet we have to learn to walk all over again."

At last, early the next morning, the captain gave the order to drop anchor.

Almost immediately a flotilla of small boats rowed out to greet them. There were reporters from the papers seeking the latest news from the States, vendors praising the virtues of this hotel or that, and, most welcome of all, two boats piled high with all manner of unfamiliar fruits.

Uncle Eli passed down some coins in a basket to a dark-skinned man in a large straw hat. He spoke rapidly in a language Luke did not recognize. "Is he speaking Spanish?" Luke asked as Uncle Eli used sign language to indicate what he wanted.

"No, that's Portuguese," explained Uncle Eli. "I can speak a little Spanish since I used to trade in Santa Fe. Portuguese is a bit similar, but not close enough for him to understand me."

In spite of the language difficulties, a bargain was soon made, and the basket was pulled over the rail. Luke liked the look of a long, yellow, curved fruit and took a bite. He quickly spit it out.

Uncle Eli laughed. "You have to peel that one before you eat." He showed Luke and Toby how to peel back the skin. Luke sniffed suspiciously. It certainly smelled good. Shrugging, he bit into the smooth, creamy inner fruit. "Mmm," he said. "This is wonderful."

"What are they called?" Toby asked.

"Bananas," Captain Andrews said when Uncle Eli could not answer. "They grow only where it is very warm."

At last a more impressive boat came alongside,

and the ladder was lowered for several officials led by a short, pompous-appearing man wearing a uniform covered with medals. He inspected their papers. Then he made the passengers and crew line up while he checked for signs of illness.

"You are fortunate," he said in a heavy accent. "The last ship had the cholera. They buried ten people at sea."

At last he went with the captain and Uncle Eli to the hold for an estimate of the duty fees.

By the time everything was pronounced in order it was late in the afternoon, and Captain Andrews announced that the first boats would not go ashore until morning.

Nearly all of the ship's company slept on deck that night. It was warm, but a cooling breeze brought the spicy scent of flowers and fruit over the water. Luke, Toby, and Jim had spread their blankets in the shadows behind the goat pens.

Uncle Eli and Colleen walked past, holding hands. "Are you ready to go ashore?" Uncle Eli asked.

Luke thought of his drawing materials carefully packed away for the shore and nodded.

"We've been talking," Colleen said. "We've noticed that you three have gotten to be good friends. Would you like to stay with us while we're onshore, Jim?"

Jim nodded eagerly. "That would be wonderful."

"I'll be busy a lot of the time arranging for new supplies," Uncle Eli said. "But there'll still be plenty of time to see the sights."

Luke, Toby, and Jim looked happily at one another. Suddenly Colleen bent down and patted the cabin boy's head. "Child, do we have to keep calling you Jim?"

Jim stammered in surprise. "W-what do you mean?"

"We've had such lovely talks while you've been helping me in the pantry. I've known for some time now that you are a girl."

Jim glanced quickly at Luke.

"We know, too," he told her. "And we know your name is 'Louisa.' "

Jim, now Louisa, put her hands on her hips. "You mean, I didn't fool anyone?"

Uncle Eli looked confused. "You fooled me."

"I don't think Captain Andrews or any of the

other passengers suspect," Toby said. "We just figured it out last week."

Louisa sat back down. "What's going to happen to me now?"

Uncle Eli smiled. "You are going to get some sleep like the rest of us. First thing in the morning we are all going onshore and having a lovely holiday. We'll worry about everything else later."

ELEVEN

—————•—————

Rio

The night seemed to last forever, but at last a red ball of light crept over the horizon. Uncle Eli, Colleen, Luke, Toby, and Louisa boarded one of the small ferries waiting to take them ashore. Uncle Eli and Colleen now knew Louisa's story, except for the secret message, and Uncle Eli had reluctantly agreed that she could continue to work as the cabin boy.

"But not while we are in Rio," Colleen declared. "I'm going to buy you a dress. I'll need a bridesmaid at my wedding."

"The first thing I want to do is mail a letter to my mother," Toby said.

"I wrote one, too," Uncle Eli said. "We'll find a ship heading back home to take them."

They walked up the street to a hotel. It was one that the vendors had told them about the day before, singing praises that turned out to be close to the truth. It was called the Santa Maria, and it was clean and comfortable. There was a courtyard with shady tables and a wild profusion of flowering trees and shrubs around the front. Brightly colored birds perched on the branches.

Rio was a large town with many impressive buildings, and even more beautiful churches. Luke noted the curious fact that the gutters were in the middle of the wide paved streets.

There were so many English-speaking people that it was easy to do business. While Colleen and Louisa went shopping, Luke and Toby went with Uncle Eli while he arranged for fresh water to be taken to the ship and for the stores of flour, sugar, and beans to be replenished. Luke and Toby enjoyed watching the negotiations. Instead of the merchant's posting a price and the customer's paying it, here buying was a game. First the merchant named a ridiculously high price. Then the customer, acting offended, offered an equally silly low price. Back and forth went the offers.

"I am a poor man," one merchant said with a sad look. "So many children to feed. They would surely starve if I sold my sugar for such a low price."

Uncle Eli pointed to the man's round belly. "You do not appear to be starving. I, on the other hand, am truly a poor man. And I would be in the poorhouse if I were to pay these prices."

"Sir, the fine cut of your clothes tells me things go well with you," said the merchant, who then named a higher price.

Finally a sum satisfied both sides. "You are a hard bargainer," the merchant said. "Fortunately for me not all from your country know how to buy. Some pay what we ask and grumble that we are trying to cheat them out of their money."

With the same sort of bargaining Colleen arranged for a dress to be made for Louisa and a wedding dress for herself.

On the morning of the wedding Luke could not believe his eyes. From the scruffy cabin boy, Louisa had been transformed into an elegant young lady.

Her dress was a shiny blue that matched her eyes, and Colleen had trimmed the ragged haircut and curled Louisa's hair by tying it with little strips of cloth. No trace remained of the dirty street urchin named Jim.

"You look beautiful," Luke said.

Louisa blushed and smoothed her skirt. "What if Captain Andrews sees me?" she asked with a worried frown.

"He won't even recognize you," Toby told her.

The wedding ceremony was held at a small church near the hotel. Captain Andrews was there along with Mr. Beardsly, the judge, Mr. Appleby, and a few other friends from the ship.

Toby was right. When Captain Andrews was introduced to Louisa Turner, the daughter of a friend, he bowed gallantly, with no sign of recognition.

"Hey," Toby said to Luke, "I just thought of something. Now you'll have to call her Aunt Colleen."

"That's right," Luke said happily. In the time he had known Colleen, he had already grown to love her.

Uncle Eli was beaming at everyone.

"I hope he doesn't get any happier," Luke said with a grin. "If he does, he might start singing."

Uncle Eli managed to get through the ceremony without breaking into one of his off-key serenades. After the wedding Luke, Toby, and Louisa went with Uncle Eli and Colleen to the botanical gardens. They spent the afternoon exclaiming in delight while a guide showed off the brilliantly colored flowers and birds. Luke was glad he had brought his sketchbook, but the pencil drawings could not capture the wonderful colors. Whenever he remembered Rio, he would think first of the bright colors.

The day before they left they discovered a small square with shops and eating places and spent several pleasant hours there. Then, noticing a crowd, they squeezed through to see what was attracting so much attention. Colleen gave a gasp, and her arm went around Toby protectively. It was a slave auction. About twenty hollow-eyed black men, women, and children were lined up while the crowd called out their bids. Uncle Eli looked grim, and he hurried them away. Later he talked with Toby for a long time.

Louisa was indignant. "How can they have all those beautiful churches and do that?" she exclaimed.

"This is a different culture," Uncle Eli answered. "And how can we criticize them when we do the same?"

Luke was shocked. Although he knew slavery existed, he had never seen such a thing. "Like that?" he asked, his voice shaking.

Uncle Eli nodded grimly. "Just like that."

Luke felt a deep shame for his country. He tried to imagine Toby and Miss Maisie being auctioned. The thought was too horrible to think about.

On the last day before they sailed again, Luke and Toby accompanied Uncle Eli as he made final arrangements for supplies to be loaded onto the ship.

"Isn't that Mr. Browning?" Toby asked.

Luke looked where Toby pointed. Half hidden behind an old storehouse close to the water's edge, Mr. Browning was deep in conversation with a rough-looking man wearing a captain's jacket.

"Maybe we'll be lucky and he'll change ships," Toby remarked.

There was something furtive about the two men's appearance.

Luke shrugged. It was too nice a day to worry about Mr. Browning. The boys hurried to catch up with Uncle Eli, and Luke put Mr. Browning out of his mind.

The next day the ferry took them back to the ship. Louisa's dress was packed away, her hair was straight again, and she had put on her duckcloth trousers and ragged shirt. She had even rubbed a little dirt on her face.

"You don't have to keep pretending. Stay with us," Uncle Eli urged her again.

Louisa shook her head. "Being a cabin boy is not so bad," she said. "And these pants are a lot more comfortable than a dress."

To Luke's great disappointment the first person he ran into after reboarding the ship was Mr. Browning. The man hurried over to Uncle Eli. "I hear congratulations are in order," he said. "I was surprised you did not have the ceremony on board ship so that all the passengers could enjoy the occasion."

Uncle Eli put his arm around Colleen. "We

wanted a small church wedding," he answered. "Rio is such a beautiful town."

"I didn't like it at all," Mr. Browning said. He stared at Louisa. "I'm surprised you preferred the company of a cabin boy to that of your passengers."

"Jim is only a child," Colleen snapped. "It would not have been safe for him alone in town."

Mr. Browning sniffed. "Oh, you're quite right," he said in an oily voice. "It's very commendable of you to take him under your wing, so to speak."

Uncle Eli brushed past Mr. Browning. "If you will excuse us, we would like to get settled," he said shortly.

"Of course," Mr. Browning said with a wide smile that did not reflect in his eyes.

"What an unpleasant man," Colleen said when he was out of hearing.

Uncle Eli nodded. "I'll be happy to see the last of him."

"Poor Mr. Appleby—," Luke began.

"Speaking of Mr. Appleby, be sure to tell him that you are ready to resume your studies."

Both boys groaned, but they nodded. Luke was

not as unhappy as he pretended to be. Mr. Appleby was a good teacher. Luke was already through the third-level reading book. It had taken him a while to get started, but now even the tutor was surprised at how fast he was progressing.

TWELVE

———•———

Pirates

After their brief holiday the passengers on the *Eagle* set out with renewed energy. It helped that the weather was good and a brisk wind kept them skimming through the waves. In a few days everyone had settled back into the daily routine.

One afternoon a ship was sighted some distance away. It followed them, never seeming to get any closer. It would disappear in the distance, then be sighted again. At first the captain showed little concern, but as the day slipped by, he paced the poop deck, George wrapped around his shoulders, and peered at the ship through his looking glass.

"Is something wrong?" Uncle Eli asked finally.

"It may be nothing," answered the captain, "but

it doesn't seem quite right the way that ship is tailing us."

Mr. Levering spoke up. "Maybe it's one of the ships that we saw at harbor in Rio, heading for California like us."

"Maybe," the captain said. "But I'm pretty sure I see cannon on her decks. I just don't like the feel of it."

Luke remembered the ship he'd seen in Rio the night they arrived—the *Neptune's Surprise*. There had been cannon on her deck. Could she be the same ship?

As evening approached, a mist rose from the sea. Captain Andrews looked pleased. "We'll lose her in the fog."

The fog thickened, muffling sounds and casting an eerie glow around the ship. Everyone was silent, straining to see though the fog. Then, when the wind blew away the fog for an instant, the sudden dark shape of a ship appeared, gliding dangerously close. Captain Andrews shouted an order at the helmsman, who turned the wheel sharply away. "Everyone below," Captain Andrews ordered, "and put out the lights."

Grumbling uneasily, the passengers did as he said.

The fog was suddenly so thick that Luke could not see his hand in front of his face. He and Toby had to feel their way along the deck.

"You boys get below," Captain Andrews said in a harsh whisper a few inches away.

"We are, sir," Toby said.

Suddenly George was thrust into Luke's arms. "Take George to my cabin boy," Captain Andrews said, still whispering. "Tell him to take good care of him or I'll thump him good."

"Yes, sir," Luke said.

Just as they reached the door, a wavering light flickered near the stern railing. "What's that?" Toby said, pointing.

"I'll take care of that," the captain growled. Muttering an oath, he headed for the stern, but the light had disappeared. Not waiting to see who it was, the boys scurried inside.

No lights could be lit in the saloon because of the skylights. Still holding George, the boys felt their way through the darkness to Louisa's tiny cabin and tapped at the door. She opened it a crack and peered out. A small whale oil lamp glowed from a corner. "I thought it would be all right since the room is closed in," Louisa explained.

Luke handed George to her, repeating the captain's orders.

"George sleeps with me sometimes," Louisa said as she held the purring cat in her arms.

"Somebody was on deck with a light," Luke said.

"Who would do that?" Louisa asked.

"Somebody pretty stupid," Luke said.

"Or a ghost," said Toby with a nervous laugh.

Luke laughed, too, but he had to admit the light had looked ghostlike. "You don't think someone was trying to signal the other ship, do you?"

They looked at one another in silence. "No," Louisa finally said. "It was probably someone who didn't hear the captain's orders."

Luke looked doubtful. "I wouldn't have wanted to be in his shoes. I'll bet the captain really yelled at him," he said.

The boys said good-night to Louisa and felt their way back to their own cabin. The passageway door to the deck opened and closed quietly, and they heard footsteps heading toward them.

"Who's there?" Toby asked nervously.

The footsteps stopped, and there was silence, as though the person were holding his breath. Then a tall figure pushed past them and hurried away without speaking. A second later they heard a door quietly close.

"Who was that?" Toby asked.

"I think it was the person who had the light," Luke answered. "His clothes were wet. I felt them when he brushed by."

"Could you tell what cabin he went into?" Toby asked.

Luke shook his head, forgetting that it was too dark for Toby to see.

The boys dared not light a lamp because their cabin had a small port window. They stumbled to their bunks and sat down. The ship was utterly silent. The fog even muffled the usual moans and creaks that were a normal part of the ship. It was a long time before Luke fell into a troubled sleep.

Morning brought good news. The fog had lifted, and a jubilant Captain Andrews announced that they had been able to evade the other ship during the long night. Several times that day he sent a sailor scrambling up the tallest mast to scan the horizon with the looking glass, but each time there was no sign of the other ship. Nothing was said about the mysterious lantern holder.

The fog seemed to have ushered in a change of weather. Now when the boys went on deck, they put on jackets. Day by day the weather grew cooler, and several times brief squalls with lightning and rolling thunder drove them below.

Once again everyone suffered from seasickness. The ship pitched and rolled, slamming into the waves so hard that it seemed a miracle that it stayed in one piece.

Captain Andrews and his men fought the sea as the ship made her way down the desolate coast toward Cape Horn. The sailors' faces were gray with weariness as they stumbled to their berths after each watch. The passengers huddled below, damp, fearful, and sick.

On milder days the passengers crowded the decks, wrapped in coats and blankets. Cold as it was, it was better than the damp, stuffy area belowdecks.

"We'd better check the animals," Luke shouted over the pounding sea one such morning.

Toby nodded. He had been sick for days, unable

to eat, and he looked pale and listless. Luke put his arm around his friend. "You sit there and get some fresh air," he said. "I'll see to them."

Toby sat gratefully in a sheltered part of the deck. "Sorry to be such a baby," he said.

The animals looked in surprisingly good shape, damp but safe under their protective canvas cover. Luke fed them quickly and had started to return to Toby when he noticed Mr. Browning leaning against the rail, peering intently at the far horizon. Suddenly Luke saw why. Mr. Browning turned slightly and noticed Luke. "There's a ship off the starboard side," he called loudly.

The sailors, scrambling across the rigging, had already seen the ship. Captain Andrews peered through his looking glass.

"Is it the same one, do you think?" asked Uncle Eli.

"Might be. I can't tell yet," the captain answered. "She's not showing her colors," he told Uncle Eli.

Several times they had seen other ships and shouted greetings and information through the captain's bullhorn. Each time the *Eagle* had run up the United States flag, showing where they were from. The other ships had done the same. However, this ship remained dark and unknown as she steadily followed.

"Do you suppose they don't see us?" Uncle Eli asked.

"They see us all right," Captain Andrews said grimly. He pointed to the topmost mast. A small figure was just barely visible.

Uncle Eli looked through the glass again. "I see four cannon," he said quietly.

Captain Andrews looked even grimmer. "Pirates," he said. "Our only hope it to stay ahead of them. This time we don't have a fog to hide in, but maybe we can outrun them tonight."

THIRTEEN

Shipwreck

The cry went through the passengers, who crowded along the rail with anxious looks. Luke returned to Toby and told him what was happening. "What are we going to do?" Toby asked.

"Captain Andrews says we're going to outrun them," Luke replied. "You know the *Eagle*'s just about the fastest ship there is."

The first mate talked in low tones to Mr. Browning, who then smiled. Luke watched them. "Mr. Browning doesn't seem very worried," he said. "He's probably friends with the pirates." He had spoken in bitter jest, but now that the words were said he wondered if they could be true. Of all the passengers, only Mr. Browning seemed unconcerned. Luke suddenly remembered the man who had squeezed by them in the dark passageway. Mr. Browning was the right size to have been that man.

Captain Andrews yelled at Mr. Levering, who hurried to take his place beside the captain. Despite the heavy seas, the sails were unfurled to make the ship run at high speed. After several hours the pirates' ship was only a dot in the distance. The passengers let out a cheer. "Hooray for the captain," they shouted.

"We're not safe yet," said the captain, pointing to the sky. "Another storm's coming."

No sooner had he spoken than it started to rain. It was so cold that as soon as the raindrops hit the decks, they froze. The planks were soon dangerously slippery. The ice froze in the sailors' beards and eyelashes.

"Get below," Uncle Eli ordered tersely.

Slipping and sliding, Luke and Toby made their way inside.

"You look frozen. Get out of those wet clothes," Colleen said. She brushed ice from their hair. "As soon as you have changed, I'll give you a cup of soup."

Luke and Toby hurried to their cabin. Just as they reached the door, Mr. Appleby slipped out. "Oh, there you are," he said cheerfully. "I made some new lessons for you. I put them on your desk." With a wave he hurried down the passage-way to his own room.

Luke groaned when he saw the stack of papers on the desk. He was too cold to think about study-ing now. Toby felt under his mattress. He looked relieved when he felt the book exactly where he had left it.

"You're not still thinking Mr. Appleby is after the message?" Luke asked as they peeled off their wet clothing and dressed again.

"I do think I left that paper folded," Toby said. Still shivering, they hurried back to the pantry. Louisa brought them a bowl of thick soup with beans and pieces of ham.

"Have we escaped the pirates?" Louisa asked.

"I certainly hope so," Colleen said. "I don't care to spend my honeymoon fighting pirates."

"Nor do I," said Uncle Eli, coming in from the storm at last. He leaned over the stove, letting the heat melt the ice in his beard, then dried his face with a towel.

Later that evening Luke was in his room trying to ignore his churning stomach and study his history lesson. Toby was curled up on his bunk, moaning in his misery. George crawled into Luke's lap and purred loudly. Now that the weather was so bad, he had abandoned the captain's quarters for the inside cabins, although they were not much warmer. Luke absentmindedly stroked the cat's head.

Louisa tapped on the door. When Luke let her in, she put a plate of cookies on the desk.

"Good news," she said. "Captain Andrews thinks we have outrun the other ship. It hasn't been sighted for several hours. Have you gotten any ideas about my father's message?" she asked.

Toby shook his head. "I've been too sick to think about it, and Mr. Appleby just gave us more schoolwork."

Louisa patted his hand. "Poor Toby."

"Uncle Eli says the sea will be worse once we reach Cape Horn, but then it will get better," Luke said.

Toby reached for a cookie and nibbled it listlessly. "These are good."

Louisa clapped her hands. "I made them," she said, obviously pleased. "Colleen showed me how."

Luke smiled at his friend. "You are amazing," he said. "You can do all the cabin boy things and have time for baking. I don't think I could even be a good cabin boy."

Louisa smiled back. "You could be a good cabin boy. All you have to do is let everyone yell at you." She paused. "Captain Andrews is a fair man. The sailors say that most captains beat their cabin boys."

The next afternoon there was a few hours' break in the weather. Anxious to get a little fresh air, passengers hurried to the decks even though their teeth were chattering. There was land in the distance, but it was rocky and wind-swept, and the only vegetation was a few stunted bushes clinging to the hills. Louisa was the first to notice something unusual floating in the water.

"Captain," she called, "it looks like a ship's mast."

As the object floated nearer, Luke saw that Louisa was right. Bits of torn sail clung to the wreckage, and the mast itself was scorched.

"Should we search for survivors?" asked Mr. Beardsly.

The captain shook his head. "Not likely to be any," he said grimly. "The ship has burned and broken apart on the rocks. If we get in closer to search, we might end up like those poor souls. Anyway, from the looks of that mast it's been in the water for days."

The passengers stood along the railing and watched the mast until it had drifted out of sight. They passed bits of debris for several hours, but there was no sign of survivors. Everyone on board was unusually silent, reminded of how perilous his or her own journey was.

Toward evening a huge fogbank rolled toward them, and once again everyone was ordered below. With the smoother seas Toby was feeling better and the boys sat on the floor of the cabin playing checkers. Even though they were inside, it was so cold their breaths made frosty steam, and between moves Luke warmed his fingertips under his arms.

Suddenly Toby stopped just as he was about to king one of Luke's men. "I don't think we're moving," he said.

Luke opened the door to their cabin and saw Mr.

Colville rushing by. "Is something wrong?" he asked.

"Ice," said Mr. Colville. "They've spotted a huge iceberg. With this fog there is a danger of running into one."

"Ice," Luke groaned. "One more thing to worry about."

"It's a sign we are near Cape Horn at last," Toby said.

"Uncle Eli says sometimes the storms are so bad that it takes ships weeks to get around," Luke said glumly.

"At least it's summer," Toby said. "Think of how awful it must be in June. That's winter here."

Luke did some quick counting on his fingers. "It's almost Christmas!" he exclaimed. "I wish I had something to give Uncle Eli and Colleen. Aunt Colleen," he added, correcting himself.

Toby frowned thoughtfully. Then he brightened. "Why don't you make them a wedding picture?"

Luke whooped happily. "You're a genius. That would be perfect." He got out his easel and paints. First he quickly sketched the happy couple. "I'll put them in the botanical garden," he said.

Toby watched, shaking his head in amazement as the picture took shape. "I wish I could do that."

"I wish I could learn Greek and Latin as quickly as you. I can barely get through English." Luke paused. "I can't remember the shape of Colleen's eyes."

"Let's go say hello," Toby said.

They found Uncle Eli and Colleen in the saloon. Uncle Eli was studying some charts. Colleen was sewing by the dim light from the whale oil lamp. She put down her sewing and greeted them.

"Is something wrong?" she asked with a worried look at Luke.

"We were just bored," he said.

Colleen poured them cups of tea, and Uncle Eli left his charts to sit with them. "Captain Andrews says there's been no sign of that other ship. He thinks it may have taken the shortcut through the Strait of Magellan. It saves several weeks of traveling, but it's a much more dangerous passage."

Luke tried to remember his geography while he was sketching. Mr. Appleby had told them that the Strait of Magellan was a narrow passage to the north of Cape Horn that had sudden, violent storms. Ships were often wrecked on the rocky coast.

"What are you drawing?" Colleen asked.

"Oh, nothing," Luke said, flipping his tablet closed. "I guess we'll go back to our cabin now."

Colleen gave them a puzzled look. "Good-night then."

"Good-night," the boys called out cheerfully.

Luke showed Toby the sketches he'd made of the couple's eyes and noses. He worked on his picture for several minutes. Then he stared thoughtfully. "Something's still not right."

Toby peered over Luke's shoulder. "Uncle Eli is perfect, but you're right about Colleen. Maybe it's her mouth."

"I need to look again," Luke said.

Back they went to the saloon. "You two again?" said Uncle Eli. "You must really be restless to-night."

"We're a little hungry," Luke said.

Colleen went to the pantry and returned with a plate of bread and some cheese. "It's goat cheese," she said. "I made it myself."

Luke took the plate and thanked her as he stared

all the while at her lips, trying to memorize each line.

"Well, good-night again," Toby said.

"Are you two up to something?" Uncle Eli said.

"Oh, no, sir," Luke said as innocently as he could manage.

"Are you worried about the cape passage?" Uncle Eli asked.

"A little," Luke said.

"Captain Andrews is an experienced captain," Uncle Eli said. "And the weather is holding up pretty well for this area. It will be a little rough, but we'll be all right."

Laughing, the boys returned to their quarters, and Luke sketched in the mouth.

"Perfect," Toby said, clapping his hands.

"Tomorrow I'll start painting it," said Luke. He rolled up the paper and tucked it behind the desk.

The morning, however, brought no chance for painting. The ship pitched and rolled in the high seas, and waves crashed across the decks. Water leaked into the cabin areas, making everything damp and miserable. Luke and Toby huddled shivering in their blankets. When the winds seemed to die down a little, they hurried out to tend the animals. To their surprise they found the deck covered with snow.

FOURTEEN

———•———

Rounding the Cape

Slipping and sliding, the boys made their way across the deck. "We could have a snowball fight," Luke said, scraping up a handful off the deck and throwing it at Toby. Laughing, his friend ducked just in time. The snowball flew onward to land squarely in the middle of the back of a man standing along the rail.

Luke froze, waiting for a scolding. But the man turned and lobbed two snowballs back at them. There followed several minutes of fast and furious snowball attacks. Suddenly Captain Andrews appeared. "Judge," he said, "I am surprised at you." Captain Andrews's face was stern, but Luke thought he saw a twinkle in his eye.

Judge Myer's face was beet red—from cold or embarrassment, Luke could not tell. "Sorry, Captain. We couldn't resist."

"Well, I suggest you all go below," the captain said. "We're starting the passage around the Horn today."

The judge winked at Luke and Toby. "I haven't had that much fun in years," he said when Captain Andrews was out of hearing. "But the captain is right. The waters off the Horn are tricky."

The boys discovered the meaning of those words over the next week. A wild wind would push them along at a good clip only to reverse itself and send the ship back to where she had been the day before. A sudden calm would be followed by violent squalls that threatened to capsize the ship. Now and then they had a glimpse of the harsh shoreline, its dangerous rocks waiting to welcome the doomed passengers of less fortunate captains. But the *Eagle* fought her way through and emerged one morning into the bright blue waters of the Pacific.

During the lulls in the weather Luke managed to finish the picture, and on Christmas morning he proudly presented it to Uncle Eli and Colleen. Luke's new aunt fixed a special breakfast that included an orange carefully hoarded since the stop in Rio. She gave Luke and Toby new shirts she had sewed during the voyage, and for Louisa there was a new dress made of cloth she had also purchased during the stop. Toby shyly presented a beautifully polished wood picture frame he had made with the help of the ship's carpenter.

The other passengers celebrated as well. There was a church service in the morning and a festive midday meal. Later Mr. Beardsly shared a sack of horehound candy he had been saving, and the ship rang with the sounds of fiddles, banjos, and tambourines. Even Mr. Browning sucked on his piece of candy and for once did not complain.

Luke fought the homesickness that pressed at him all day. He sat quietly listening to the music, thinking about his brothers, Caleb and Michael, and his twin sisters, Mary Alice and Catherine Louise, at home so far away. He wondered if they missed him or if they were too busy enjoying life in town. Next spring the family would go back to the farm and start over. Even though he hated the farm, Luke couldn't help wishing he were there. He saw from the look on Toby's face how much he was missing his mother. Holidays seemed to make it worse.

As if she had read their thoughts, Colleen came over and put her arms around them. "There's something about Christmas that makes us miss our families even more," she said. "I'm thinking of my mam and brother this day."

Luke had never thought of Colleen having a family. "Do you miss them a lot?" he asked.

Colleen wiped her eyes with the back of her hand. "That I do," she said softly. Then she suddenly brightened. "Your uncle and I are thinking of making a family ourselves."

"You're going to have a baby?" Luke exclaimed.

Colleen laughed. "No, no. Not yet at any rate. No, we were thinking about Louisa. She has no family, and I've grown very fond of her."

"That's a great idea," Luke said.

"Do you think she'll agree?" Colleen asked.

Luke thought. "She's pretty stubborn. But she loves you, too. I think she will."

"Good," Colleen said. "We'll talk to her in a few

days. In the meantime, keep this to yourselves. Now come dance with me."

Colleen whirled them around in a lively jig. It was almost sunrise before the Christmas celebration ended and everyone stumbled off to sleep. The long night made it easy to sleep through the sudden squall that rose the next day. Toby slept so soundly he didn't even complain of seasickness.

The Pacific side of the continent had not brought any great improvement in the weather. Captain Andrews carefully guided the ship through several ice fields, and day after day the passengers were forced to stay below because of sudden storms. But slowly the weather improved, and although the air was still cool, they no longer shivered when they went on deck.

"Will we just sail straight up the coast?" Luke asked Mr. Appleby during their geography lesson.

Mr. Appleby spread a map of the world on the desk. "We'll follow the coast for a while," he said. "But then we'll sail far to the west, nearly to the Hawaiian Islands. That way we can pick up the winds to send us to California."

Luke and Toby looked with dismay at the

distance they still had to travel. Although Mr. Appleby assured them it would go quickly, they were not sure they could stand many more weeks of boredom aboard ship.

A few mornings later Luke, Toby, and Louisa were taking the goats for a walk around the deck to give them some exercise. They had all become fond of the goats. The smallest was Maggie, and next was Katie. The largest goat Luke named Daisy because she had a spot on her head that looked just like a flower. They had discovered that with a rope tied loosely around each animal's neck the goats would follow them around almost like pet dogs. George did not approve of such goings-on and usually retreated to Captain Andrews's shoulder, from where he watched with disdainful interest. They had marched around the deck several times when Louisa suddenly sniffed the air. "What's that terrible smell?"

Luke breathed in and then coughed. The air had a sharp smell of ammonia.

"That's bird waste you're smellin'," one of the sailors informed them. "We're passing the Guano Islands." He jerked his thumb toward several small

islands just barely visible in the distance. A faint yellow mist seemed to surround them.

"They use it for fertilizer," the sailor said. "Prisoners and Chinamen dig it up, poor devils. Then they ship it on barges."

As the *Eagle* passed the islands, they could see men with picks loosening chunks of the waste, or guano, on the top of the rocks. Below in a small cove was a ship at anchor. The men loaded the chunks into wheelbarrows and dumped them into what looked like canvas chutes leading to the ship's hold.

Luke sprinkled some corn for the goats and leaned on the rail to watch. Even from this distance the smell made his eyes water. He felt terrible pity for the men who were forced to work this way. He stared at the islands glumly until they had passed out of sight.

"We forgot the goats," Toby said suddenly.

Luke whirled around in dismay. The nimble-footed goats had managed to escape from the main deck. Daisy was standing on the poop deck calmly chewing the canvas cover for the skylights.

Captain Andrews noticed at the same instant.

"What is this animal doing loose on my ship?" he roared.

"Sorry, sir," Luke called. "We'll get them right now." Maggie was nearby. Louisa managed to catch her and get her back in the pen. Luke and Toby raced for Katie, but just as they reached her, the goat jumped back to the main deck and managed to evade capture.

Captain Andrews watched with hands on his hips. "Get those animals off my deck," he said in a tight, angry voice. Daisy suddenly popped up in front of Luke, who made a desperate grab. He managed to grab only a handful of hair as his foot slipped on the wet plank, and he fell with a crash.

By now several passengers had come on deck to see what was happening. They laughed loudly as the children raced around the decks, the goats scampering just out of reach.

"You go that way and I'll circle," Toby said, pointing to Katie, now back on the main deck. Carefully they encircled the goat, who this time calmly waited for capture. Louisa took her back to the safety of the pen.

Daisy proved to be the hardest to catch. Time

and again they thought she was cornered, only to have her slip away at the last minute. The passengers were enjoying the spectacle immensely, but the captain's face grew redder by the minute. At last they had Daisy trapped against the poop deck rail.

She bleated piteously. "Come on, you silly thing," Louisa crooned. "I'll give you some corn."

Daisy took one step toward them. But then she seemed to change her mind. She twisted her body and seemed to be trying to climb the railing. Toby lunged forward to catch her, but before Luke realized what was happening Daisy had slipped under the rail and tumbled out of sight.

FIFTEEN

—◆—

Attack!

"Goat overboard!" a sailor sang out. "Shall we fetch it back, Captain?"

Captain Andrews sighed. "Launch the longboat."

Luke stared over the rail at the helpless goat. Instinctively Daisy knew how to swim, but her struggles were tiring her in the icy water, and she was falling behind.

"Hurry," he cried.

"Don't worry, lad. We'll get her," said one of the sailors.

Then there was a groan from the passengers who had rushed to watch the rescue. "Shark," called Mr. Colville.

Luke saw it, too: a dark shape circling the

defenseless goat. Daisy gave one sharp bleat, and she was gone. There was a frenzy of fins and tails. A red stain spread, then washed away, and the water was deadly calm.

The silence was broken only by a sob from Louisa.

"Stop your blubbering, boy," Captain Andrews said harshly. "You've lost a valuable piece of cargo. Maybe a whipping will help you learn responsibility."

Uncle Eli stepped forward. "There will be no whipping. The children loved that goat. They've had punishment enough."

"The cabin boy is part of my crew. I decide how my men are punished," the captain said furiously. He roared so loudly that George jumped down and crouched fearfully under the wheelhouse.

"This child is under my protection," Uncle Eli said. "She has agreed to let me be her guardian."

"*She?*" spluttered the captain.

Colleen stepped over and put her arm around Louisa. "Yes, Captain. Your cabin boy is really a girl."

The passengers buzzed with the news. Captain Andrews stared. He turned away abruptly. "That girl in Rio. I thought she looked familiar," he said.

"Wait," Louisa suddenly blurted out. "I'd like to keep on being the cabin"—she hesitated—"girl."

Captain Andrews shook his head. "I don't like being tricked. And whoever heard of a cabin girl?"

"I didn't mean to trick you," Louisa said. "I needed a job. I'm still the same person. Haven't I always done a good job for you?"

Captain Andrews gave her a hard stare. "All right then. Go fetch me a cup of tea, Jim." He shook his head. "What is your name?"

"Louisa, sir. I'll get your tea right now," she answered, scurrying to the galley.

Captain Andrews shook his head again. "A girl," he mumbled.

Still stunned by Daisy's sudden death, Luke turned back to the ocean. He knew he would never be able to care for Maggie and Katie without remembering the terrible price of a moment of carelessness. From Toby's stricken face, Luke knew his friend felt the same way.

The next day was warm but rainy.

"Mr. Levering has sailed this coast before. He knows of an island with a protected cove to anchor the *Eagle*," Uncle Eli said. "We'll go ashore and get some fresh water and fruit." This was good news. The stores of fruits and vegetables had long ago been eaten or spoiled, and the water was once again turning rancid.

The boys looked eagerly as the ship sailed into the harbor. It was a small island but thickly forested. Gorgeously colored birds screeched out an alarm as they circled the trees.

That night Luke and Toby were too excited to sleep. They had long since finished their homework and spent several hours playing chess, which Toby won, as usual.

"Am I ever going to beat you?" Luke groaned.

"You're getting better," Toby said, laughing. "Maybe someday."

Luke threw his pillow at his friend, and for a few minutes they wrestled in the cramped quarters of their cabin. At last they sat quietly, and Toby pulled out the now-grimy paper with the mysterious message.

They had spent hours writing the letters backward, checking the words in the book where the dots were found, and looking for patterns in the arrangements of letters. Nothing made the message clear.

"I thought maybe it had something to do with the page numbers," Toby said. "But nothing makes any sense."

Luke stretched out on his bunk and yawned. It seemed as though he had just barely closed his eyes, but when he awoke, the sun was already high in the sky.

Luke jumped into his clothes. "Hurry up."

Toby groaned and sat up. "I didn't mean to sleep so late. I hope the boats didn't go without us," he said. He picked up the paper from the desk where he had placed it the night before.

"After all this work it will probably turn out to be something simple like moving every letter three places," he said lazily. Then he froze.

Luke counted the alphabet on his fingers. "You mean, like A equals D?"

Toby stared at him for a minute. Then he let out a shout and pounded Luke on the back. "That's it." He hit his hand on his head. "Why didn't I think of that before? It's so easy. All we have to do is count *back* three letters."

"Do you really think that might be it?" Luke asked.

Toby grabbed a pencil. "Let's find out."

Toby quickly wrote the alphabet. Then he counted carefully. "This first G would be D if we are right," he said. His forehead furrowed in concentration. "Next the H would be E. D is A and then U would be R." "Yippie," Luke shouted. "It's the word 'dear.' This has got to be right." Toby grinned back happily. "Louisa will be so happy."

A few minutes later both boys stared excitedly at the paper. *DeardaughtersickdeedtogoldisatSacramentopostofficecomeatonce.*

Toby read it aloud. " 'Dear daughter . . . sick . . . deed to gold is at Sacramento post office . . . come at once.' "

"We've got to tell Louisa!" Luke exclaimed.

"Wait," Toby called. "I'm not dressed."

"This can't wait," Luke called back. He raced to Louisa's cabin and knocked on the door, but there was no answer.

He looked quickly through the passageway and the pantry, but there was no sign of his friend. Perhaps she was on deck helping with some chore. Luke raced up the stairs and on deck.

The ship seemed nearly deserted. Most of the passengers, it seemed, were already onshore. Finally he spied Colleen enjoying the sun after the days of rain.

"Where's Louisa?" he shouted.

"She's already onshore," Colleen answered. "Why all the excitement? The boat will be coming back for us soon."

Luke tried to hide his disappointment that he would have to wait to share his wonderful news.

"I'll go tell Toby to hurry," he said.

Suddenly there were loud, cracking noises coming from the island. Colleen jumped up. "Saints preserve us, what was that?"

Luke hurried to the side and peered intently at the island. He could just make out some tiny figures that appeared to be the passengers from the *Eagle*. They were standing in small groups. A few ran across the sandy beach. Suddenly there was another crack! and Luke saw one of the figures fall.

"I think someone's attacking them," he gasped.

"Go get your uncle," Colleen said, rushing to the railing. "He's below looking at the captain's charts."

Just then the passageway door opened, and Uncle Eli stepped out. "What's going on? What's that noise? It sounds almost like gunfire."

Mr. Appleby rushed to the rail. "Someone's attacking the men onshore," he said, wringing his hands. "We have to sail away before they get us, too."

Uncle Eli looked angry. "We can't just sail away and leave all those men. At any rate most of the crew is onshore."

"What shall we do, then?" asked Mr. Appleby.

"I'm not giving up this ship without a fight," said Uncle Eli.

"I'm very disappointed to hear you say that," said a hated voice. Mr. Browning and Mr. Levering stepped around a corner. In Mr. Browning's hands was a small silver pistol.

SIXTEEN

Shark

"I'll see you hanged if any of my passengers are hurt," Uncle Eli said.

Mr. Browning shrugged. "You'll have to catch me first. But don't worry. As long as you cooperate, no one will be hurt."

"Why are you doing this?" Luke asked.

Mr. Browning shrugged. "Money, of course. Mr. Pembrook hired me to find his ward, Louisa. He suspected she might know where her father's gold was. I found out she was on the *Eagle*, and your uncle here was kind enough to allow me visit my 'poor sick brother.' " Mr. Browning chuckled. "I listened to enough of your conversations to know the girl didn't have a clue where the gold was. So there I was, a long ocean voyage for nothing. When Mr.

Levering and I met Captain Blackburn, it seemed as though fate was playing right into our hands. We decided to take over the ship and sell the goods ourselves."

Luke remembered the scruffy-looking captain he'd seen talking to Mr. Browning when they were in Rio. He bristled with anger, but Uncle Eli gave him a warning look, and Luke stayed silent.

"What does Captain Blackburn get out of all this?" Uncle Eli asked.

"Why, the ship, of course. The *Neptune's Surprise* badly needs repair."

"How did you know he was on the island?" Colleen asked.

"We arranged it in Rio, dear lady," Mr. Browning said. "Captain Blackburn was to try to overtake the ship. Barring that, he was to slip through the strait and get ahead of the *Eagle*. Then all he had to do was come here and wait. There's another small cove on the other side of the island. It's a perfect place to hide."

"So it was you," Luke blurted out. "You were on deck that foggy night signaling the *Neptune's Surprise*."

Mr. Browning just smiled.

"Just what did you intend to do with the passengers?" Uncle Eli asked bitterly.

There was another smattering of gunfire. Luke fought a rising panic. Louisa was on that island.

Mr. Browning waved his pistol. "Go see who's left on the ship. Lock them in the hold so they don't cause any problems," he said to his friend.

Mr. Appleby blanched. "There're rats down there."

Mr. Levering reached under his shirt and pulled out his own pistol, which had been hidden inside his waistband. He pointed it at Mr. Appleby, motioning for him to walk in front. "Let's hope they're not hungry," he said with a leer.

Mr. Browning turned back to Luke and his uncle. "To answer your question, we intend to leave you all on the island. We're not as bad as you seem to think. The island has plenty of food and water. Eventually a ship will come along and rescue you. In the meantime the captain changes the name of the ship, and Mr. Levering and I change our names and disappear to live out our days in comfort." A crafty look passed over Mr. Browning's face. "It seems we get a bonus. From what I've overheard, we've found the gold after all. Too bad Mr. Pembrook won't ever get any of it." He pointed to the paper. "Hand it over."

Luke groaned inwardly. How could he have been so stupid? If he had just not acted so excited, Louisa might have at least been able to keep her gold mine. He tried to slide the note in his pocket. "This is nothing. We were just playing a game."

"A game?" said Mr. Browning. "I think not. Hand over that paper."

"No," Luke said. He tossed the note over the rail. In silence the three of them watched it slowly drift down to the water.

"You little brat," Mr. Browning snarled. With his free hand he struck Luke across the face.

Luke staggered back and fell to his knees. His head was spinning. He was only half aware of Uncle Eli's leap toward the other man and the brief struggle. There was a sudden loud noise just as Luke regained his feet.

Uncle Eli had crumpled to the ground near the railing. A spot of blood was spreading rapidly on his shoulder. With one quick step Mr. Browning crossed the space between them, and while Luke watched, too terrified to move, Mr. Browning gave Uncle Eli a hard kick that sent him sliding under the rail and over the edge. A second later there was a splash as he hit the water.

Luke was aware of Colleen's scream. There was a stack of lumber near the wheel. The carpenter had been planning to make a new cover for the wheel-house. Luke shoved with all his might at the wood, sending several pieces over the edge. Then, before anyone could stop him, he threw himself over.

The height of his dive sent Luke plunging deep into the ocean. The shock of cold water nearly took his breath away. When he surfaced several seconds later, he saw Uncle Eli bobbing helplessly a few yards away. The pieces of lumber floated around them.

Luke managed to grab only two pieces before the others were swept away. They were good boards, though, flat and fairly wide. He pushed them together and paddled hard toward his uncle. The weight of his feet made it difficult to swim. Twisting his body, he kicked off his shoes, giving himself more freedom to move. Then he wiggled out of his trousers, but these he did not allow to fall free. Instead he used them to fasten the boards crudely together. By the time he reached his uncle he had a small, shaky raft.

Uncle Eli groaned. "I don't think I can make it. Leave me and head for the shore."

Luke shook his head. "I can't do that. We'll make it together."

Uncle Eli struggled weakly in the water. Luke grabbed his shirt and helped him slide up so that the boards were under his chest and head. "Hang on," he said. Taking a deep breath, he ducked under. He tugged at Uncle Eli's boots. It took several dives and gulps of air before he was able to loosen them. Gasping, he popped up one more time.

Uncle Eli groaned.

"Are you in a lot of pain?" Luke asked worriedly. He eyed the spreading spot of blood on his uncle's shirt with alarm.

"Not pain," Uncle Eli said, trying to joke. "I was just thinking about my new fifty-dollar boots heading for the bottom of the sea."

Luke grinned. "Oops. Now I need your pants. Can you loosen them?"

Uncle Eli groaned and reached to unfasten his trousers.

Luke looked back at the *Eagle*. They had drifted some distance away from the ship. He wondered what was happening to Colleen and Toby. And Mr. Appleby, he thought, ashamed that he had ever suspected him.

There was no time to worry about that now. Taking another breath, he dived under and tugged off Uncle Eli's pants. After coming up on the other side of the little raft, he used the pants to tie that end of the boards together. The makeshift raft was too small to get Uncle Eli completely out of the water, but it kept his head and shoulders out so he could float.

Luke gave a worried look at the reddish stain in the water. He wiggled out of his shirt and pressed it against his uncle's wound. Then, pushing the raft toward the island, he paddled his feet with every bit of his strength. It would be a long, hard swim, but he thought he could make it. He aimed the little raft farther around the island, hoping they would not be seen. The shore was rocky there, but he thought he could see a narrow strip of sand.

Luke swam for a while. It was farther than he thought. Uncle Eli helped at first, kicking his feet, which dangled over the side of the raft. Then he grew quiet, and Luke feared he was unconscious. Uncle Eli's face was pinched and white. A moan escaped from his lips.

Luke was growing exhausted. The water was cold, and his legs felt numb. His uncle seemed to be slipping off the boards. Treading water, Luke tried to tug at his uncle's body, but it was too heavy. Luke eyed the shore. They still had a long distance to go.

Uncle Eli's eyes opened. "Leave me," he gasped. "You'll never make it with me."

Luke shook his head. "I'm not leaving you." He paddled furiously, heading for the far-off shore. Now that he was around the cove he could see the tall spire of a mast through the rocks. The mast did not stand straight up but seemed to be bobbing off to one side. The water was suddenly filled with debris, and he realized what he was seeing. It was the *Neptune's Surprise*. It must have run aground against the rocks. Now the pounding surf was breaking her completely apart. A large piece of lumber drifted close by, and Luke grabbed at it. It might have been part of a table, for it was nearly six feet long and polished smooth. It was wide enough to hold them both, Luke thought as he eyed it for size.

He maneuvered the table close to his makeshift raft. He could see that he was just in time. The raft was falling apart, and his uncle's body had slipped even farther down into the water.

Luke leaned across the table and grasped his uncle's leg with one hand and his arm with another. "Uncle Eli," he called softly, "can you hear me?"

Uncle Eli opened his eyes, but they seemed weak and unfocused. "You have to help me," Luke pleaded. "I'm going to try to get you onto this bigger raft."

Uncle Eli nodded slightly. Luke counted. "One, two, *three*." On the last count he tugged with every bit of his remaining strength. Uncle Eli rolled off the smaller makeshift raft onto the table.

Gasping with the effort, Luke still allowed himself a moment of satisfaction. Uncle Eli was squarely on the table. Now, if he could only get himself on it without tipping them over...

He tried to climb up, but each time the table tipped, threatening to pitch Uncle Eli into the sea. He looked at the old raft, still bobbing alongside, and had an idea. If he could get aboard that, he thought he could roll over carefully enough to keep the table from tipping over. Then he could use one of the boards as an oar. He pushed the raft under his torso and, after a second to catch his breath, rolled over onto the table.

The raft swayed dangerously, nearly tipping, but at last it straightened. With a sigh of relief Luke slowly sat up. He grabbed Uncle Eli's pants, untied them, and managed to free one of the boards from the old raft.

They had drifted nearly out of sight of the cove. When he sat up, however, Luke saw something that made his heart pound with fear. Men were climbing aboard the longboat. Even at this distance Luke could tell that several were holding guns, which they held pointed at the people ashore. Luke thought of Colleen and Toby still on the ship. What would happen to them when the pirates took over? Then he had another thought. With several men rowing, it would take only a few minutes to reach the end of the cove. Concentrating on their prisoners, the pirates had not yet seen him. When the pirates were free of the cove, however, he would be in plain sight. He rowed even harder.

Perhaps if he had not been watching the pirates so closely, he might have noticed the dark shape circling the raft even sooner. As it was, the first indication he had was when the makeshift raft was bumped violently from underneath, nearly capsizing them. Luke grabbed the raft and his uncle at the same time.

"What was that?" he cried out loud.

A minute later his question was answered by the dark flash of a dorsal fin cutting through the water.

Luke looked desperately toward the shore. It was still much too far away, and the shark was between them and the beach. Luke knew they could not survive many more attacks like that. The next time the shark might tip them over. He looked at the spot of blood on his uncle's shoulder. It had dripped onto the raft, and the waves had washed the scent into the water.

Suddenly he had an idea. He took Uncle Eli's pants, which he had thrown on the raft, and rubbed them on his uncle's wound. Then, getting to his knees, he threw them as far away from the raft as he could.

There was a black streak, and suddenly the pants were yanked violently under the water. Luke didn't pause to watch. Taking the board, he pushed the raft toward the shore.

But the pants bought him only a few seconds. Luke had gained just a few yards when the shark suddenly appeared again. Fearfully Luke watched as the shark raced toward the raft. He could see the gaping mouth and the rows of daggerlike teeth. They were going to die, and there was nothing he could do.

Suddenly Luke was gripped by a terrible anger. "No," he screamed. "I'm not going through all this to be your dinner." Raising the board, he waited until he could almost smell the shark's breath. Then he swung with a force born of his rage and landed his blow right on the shark's beady cold eye.

The shark fell away as though stunned, but not before his teeth had made a painful gash on Luke's leg. He was bleeding, but there was no time to worry about that. He didn't know how much time the blow had gained him, but he knew for certain the shark would be back. His only chance was to get the raft into water too shallow for the shark to follow. His arms worked faster than he would have believed possible, and the raft shot through the water. The tides helped him now as the waves rocked them toward the shore. Using his board, he guided the raft between two large boulders and sobbed with relief at the calm, protected waters on the other side.

SEVENTEEN

Taking Back the *Eagle*

Somehow Luke managed to drag his uncle onto the beach. He took Uncle Eli's shirt off and examined the wound. The bullet had entered the fleshy part of Uncle Eli's chest and come out the other side under his arm. The bleeding had nearly stopped, and Luke thought his uncle would recover if he could get him some help. His own wound was nasty-looking and painful but would heal. Luke tore the shirt into strips and bandaged both of them as best he could.

The sun beat down on their bare skin, and Luke knew they would soon burn. He went a short way into the thick forest and tore off enough branches and leaves to make a crude shelter. His leg throbbed, but he tried to ignore the pain.

Not far from the beach he found a bubbling spring of cool, clear water. He drank eagerly and looked for a way to carry water to his uncle. He noticed a small tree laden with some kind of fruit. One of them had fallen on a rock and cracked open. It was covered with a fuzzy brown skin, but the inside was white. Using the shell as a cup, he dipped out some water for his uncle.

Uncle Eli opened his eyes. "Where are we?" he asked, struggling to sit up.

Luke gently pushed him down. "We're safe. For now, at least."

Uncle Eli looked confused. "How did we get here? Last I remember we were in the water." He frowned. "We were on some sort of raft."

Luke smiled. "I'll tell you about it later. Right now I'm going to find the others."

"Be careful," Uncle Eli said.

Luke limped off through the trees in the direction of the cove. It took only a few minutes by land to circle the island. Luke ducked down and crept through the tall grass, watching for any sign of the pirates.

The passengers and crew were sitting listlessly

on the beach. Several appeared wounded, but none seriously. Mr. Beardsly and the judge were tending to them. There was no sign of any of the pirates.

Luke looked for Louisa and finally found her sitting by herself at the edge of the beach. She was wearing her cabin boy clothes, and Luke thought she might have been crying.

Finally he stepped into sight of the people on the beach. Louisa was the first to see him. "It's Luke," she cried. She ran to him and gave him a hug.

Luke was embarrassed, but he hugged her back. "Are the pirates all gone?" he asked.

Louisa nodded. "They left some time ago. They robbed everybody and left us here. We thought you were still on the ship."

"I was," Luke said. He quickly told his adventures.

Mr. Beardsly and the judge cheered when Luke told about the shark.

"I never heard of such a thing," Mr. Colville said. "I'm going to take you fishing with me the next time. If I catch a big fish, you can hit it over the head for me."

"Luke, you're so brave!" Louisa exclaimed.

Luke squirmed under the praise. "I'm not brave. I was scared to death."

"Being brave doesn't mean you are not afraid," the judge said. "It just means doing what needs to be done even if you are afraid."

Several men left to get Uncle Eli. Luke sat on the sand and allowed himself to relax. The *Eagle* was still where they had left it, and loud laughter drifted across the bay.

"I think they found that keg of rum in the hold," Mr. Beardsly said.

"Aunt Colleen's still on the ship. And Toby," Luke whispered.

Mr. Beardsly looked pained. "There's nothing we can do, Luke."

Luke looked at the sky. It was almost dusk. The pirates were partying now, but they would surely sail at first light. What would happen to Colleen and Toby then? He shuddered at the thought of what the pirates might do.

"There has got to be something we can do. Maybe we can sneak back on the ship while they're all drunk and take back the ship."

Mr. Beardsly shook his head. "It's too far out. We couldn't swim."

"You could build rafts the way I did. There is plenty of wood on the old pirate ship. Once it's dark they wouldn't see us coming."

Mr. Beardsly stood up. "He's right, men. We could do it."

"They have guns," someone said.

"And we have clear heads," said the judge. "Are we going to let this young boy be the only brave one?"

There were calls of "He's right" and "Let's do it."

"I for one do not want to sit here on this island for months waiting for a ship," said Mr. Colville.

Quickly the passengers organized into teams and went off to search the wreckage for anything usable to make a raft. A second group set to work making some crude weapons, clubs and roughly shaped spears. In the meantime the men had found Uncle Eli and carried him to a spot close to the other wounded.

Uncle Eli was much more clearheaded in spite of his ordeal. Forgetting his wound, he pounded his fist on the ground. "If those men have harmed

Colleen or Toby..." he said. He didn't finish his threat, but his face was dark.

The men came back with the things they had salvaged, and for the next few hours the beach hummed with activity. In the meantime the noise from the *Eagle* grew even louder. They could hear laughter and loud singing and an occasional gunshot.

Luke dozed, exhausted from the day's adventure. When he awoke, he saw Uncle Eli sitting up straight, staring out at the water. His face was tight with worry. Luke could see the glow from the ship's lamps, but it was quieter now. Perhaps the pirates were asleep.

"Where are the men?" Luke asked.

"They left about an hour ago," Louisa said. "They should be almost there."

It was agonizing to sit and wait. Luke listened for the sounds of a fight, but there was only silence. Then suddenly he heard gunshots, five of them in quick succession.

Uncle Eli yelled, "That's the signal. They've taken the ship back." He raised his arm in excitement and then winced. "Oh, I got so happy I forgot about my injury." He sank back in his bed of leaves on the sand and groaned. In spite of his happy yell, Uncle Eli continued to stare out over the ocean, and Luke knew he was still worried about Colleen and Toby.

Luke suddenly looked at Louisa. "Oh, my gosh. You don't even know yet. We figured out the message. You really do have a gold mine. The deed is at the Sacramento post office." Luke quickly explained how they had figured out the message.

Louisa managed a smile. "Do you suppose I'm rich?"

"Maybe." Luke looked at the sky above. A faint streak of light lit up the horizon, but early-morning mist hid the *Eagle*.

"Ahoy there on the island. Can you hear me? It's Beardsly."

"We're here," Luke and Louisa shouted.

A minute later they could see the longboat cutting through the mist, and a minute after that they were nearly smothered by Colleen hugging them so hard that Uncle Eli yelped in pain.

"Are you all right?" Uncle Eli asked.

"I'm fine," Colleen said. "They locked me in the

hold with the other passengers. Poor Mr. Appleby was beside himself, but Captain Andrews found a lantern and got it lit, so at least it wasn't dark."

"What about Toby?" Luke asked. "Is he all right?"

"They made Toby run and fetch more rum all night. He was scared and tired, but they didn't harm him."

"I didn't even hear any fighting," Uncle Eli remarked.

"Wasn't any." Mr. Beardsly laughed. "They were all either passed out or so sound asleep they didn't even hear us coming. Captain Andrews has got them all tied up on the deck. Says he's going to deliver them to the authorities at the next port. Mr. Levering and Mr. Browning, too."

Toby was waiting for them when they reached the *Eagle*. "Everyone is talking about how brave you were saving Uncle Eli and bashing that shark," he said to Luke.

"I guess it sounds pretty brave to hear it told," Luke said. "But probably if I had taken enough time to think about what I was doing, I wouldn't have been quite so brave."

"What does Uncle Eli say about your gold mine?" Luke asked Louisa later when things had settled down.

"As soon as he sells the goods off the ship, we all are going to Sacramento to find out," answered Louisa. "He says not to get too excited because most mines play out pretty quickly. It's been so long now that maybe claim jumpers have been there. Even if it's good, he's going to make me put everything in a good bank for when I get older. In the meantime I am going to stay with him and Colleen."

"I'm glad," Luke said.

As soon as they were back on the ship, Colleen cleaned Uncle Eli's wound and put on fresh bandages and tucked him in bed. "And you're going to stay there until I say you can get up," she said.

Uncle Eli mumbled something about bossy women, but he did as he was told.

As Colleen cleaned Luke's wound, Uncle Eli opened his eyes. "I've been thinking," he said. "I must be the luckiest man in the world. Colleen is beautiful and bossy, Louisa is rich, Luke is talented, and Toby is smart. On top of that, you all are the toughest, bravest people I have ever known."

Colleen chuckled. "All that flattery and none for yourself?"

Uncle Eli grinned. "Eli Reed. Best singer in the world." He hummed a song so far out of tune that everyone laughed.

Later that night Luke lay awake listening to the soft sound of Toby's sleep. He thought about the kind of adventure that might face them in California. He thought about bravery, the sort that carried you through in times of danger and the sort his parents had as they stubbornly fought to tame the prairie. America was full of brave people, people who did what needed to be done no matter what. Uncle Eli thought that someday California would be a state. What a great country that would be, stretching from ocean to ocean. Best of all, he, Luke Reed, was going to be a part of it.

More about
Luke on the High Seas

Clipper ships were an American invention. With narrow hulls, taller masts, and more sails, they were the fastest and most graceful of all the sailing ships.

For the gold seekers on the East Coast, the clippers seemed like the perfect means to transport themselves and their equipment to California.

Advertisements promised luxurious accommodations and delicious meals, and thousands paid between three hundred and one thousand dollars for their fares.

Most travelers were not long at sea before they began to wish they had taken the overland route. Passengers suffered from seasickness, intense heat in the tropics, and terrible storms around Cape Horn. In between were weeks of boredom. And the delicious meals? After several weeks at sea the flour and beans became infested with bugs, and the water stored in wooden barrels became slimy and warm. How welcome the stops along the coast of Brazil or on a small island must have been. Here was a chance to walk on land, bring fresh water onboard, and fill up on the abundant fresh fruit.

Most men traveling to the goldfield formed companies whose members promised to help one another and to share work and expenses. Some of these companies had very strict rules governing behavior, and some tried to break the monotony of the long sea voyages with newsletters, band concerts, lectures, and church services. Once they had reached the West Coast, however, most of these companies fell apart and it was every man for himself.

The captain was master over everyone, passenger and crew alike. He spent most of his time on the poop deck, issuing orders and watching over his ship. He had to be tough. Most of his crew were wild, ignorant men who feared no man or weather and understood no law but force.

The sailor's life was rough. Sailors worked for about twelve hours each day. Their quarters were even more cramped than the second-class passengers' and were home to all kinds of vermin, like fleas, cockroaches, bedbugs, and rats. Their beds were rough board bunks with a straw-stuffed sack for a mattress. In addition, since waves often washed over the forecastle deck (at the front of the ship), the sailors' quarters were almost always damp.

While the men worked in shifts, the captain was in charge all the time. He was often rewarded with a bonus of from three thousand to five thousand dollars if the ship made the trip in less than a hundred days. Even so, many ships never made it. They were capsized during storms or dashed to pieces along the rocky shore of Cape Horn with all hands lost. Cholera and other diseases often took a terrible toll. Still, hundreds of ships did reach California. Many of them were then abandoned by crews anxious to join the diggings.

The clipper ships were successful until about 1855. The Gold Rush ended and the slower yet more reliable steamships became more common. When the transcontinental railroad was finished in 1869, the days of the great sailing ships were over.

Here are some interesting facts for you.

In this story the captain spent most of his time on the poop deck. That probably seems like a strange name. It comes from the Latin word *puppis*, which means "stern (back) of a ship."

Uncle Eli's stateroom opens onto a large, comfortably furnished *saloon*. Aboard cargo ships, the saloon is where officers and other people of high rank meet to have meals and to socialize.

The passengers on the *Eagle* were happy to have dandy funk. Another treat from that time was plum duff. It was a kind of pudding made with raisins or prunes, flour, fat, and molasses boiled in a bag. Is it any wonder that the passengers and crew were thrilled to see land and have a chance to eat fresh fruits and vegetables?

When the *Eagle* passed the Guano Islands (really the Chincha Islands) of Peru, did you know why they were called that? Guano is bird droppings! For thousands of years large seabirds nested on these islands. Because it seldom rained, the guano dried until sometimes it was over a hundred feet thick. It was a good fertilizer, and until the invention of modern fertilizers, farmers in America and England bought thousands of tons of it every year. Hundreds of Chinese workers were tricked into coming to work on these islands. Once there, they were used like slaves and treated horribly. Many committed suicide when they could not bear the terrible conditions.

Most South American countries were settled by the Spanish. But Rio de Janeiro is in Brazil, a country that was settled by the Portuguese. In those days Portugal was a major power.

Do you think you would have liked to join the Gold Rush? A few men made fortunes digging gold, but most did not. The real fortunes were made by men like Uncle Eli and others who sent for their families and stayed to build cities and a brand-new state.

DATE			